SEASONING

THE

BLADE

DIANNA
MACKINNON
HENNING

Lucky Bat Books

A Lucky Bat Book

Seasoning the Blade

Cover Artist:
Judd Lamphere
http://www.juddlamphere.com
Cover Model:
Shannon Leggett, great granddaughter to the real Ella
who inspired the story
Cover Design:
Nuno Moreira
http://www.nmdesign.org

Published by Lucky Bat Books
LuckyBatBooks.com

10 9 8 7 6 5 4 3 2 1

ISBN: 978-1-939051-60-8

This book also available in digital formats.

Discover other titles by the author at
http://www.diannahenning.com

CONTENTS

ACKNOWLEDGMENTS

Readers to whom I am most thankful: Jody Wright, Mimi Rena, Shannon Leggett, Marjie Lattka, Manjula Leggett, Hannah Tangeman-Cheney, Susannah MacKinnon Henning, Kay Oring, Beth Lerer, John O'Hearn, Lynda Jackson, Sean Henning, Miriam Aiken, Sarah Henning, members of The Thompson Peak Writers' Workshop and Sydney Ey. A big thank you also to all my friends here in Lassen County whose friendship warmed me while I wrote and revised this.

Also, a warm thank you to my son Kris Henning who suggested a stronger beginning for the book, and to Joelle Fraser for her editing suggestions.

—For the People of the Miramichi; for my Family
and for my Friends—

WEST BRANCH

There is a quiet little village
Where the winding river glows,
And there is something so majestic
As upon its way it goes
Oh this little place is West Branch
With its smiling faces fair,
Where true hearts are all united
And in pleasure all do share
And how often have I wandered
With friends beneath the willow tree so tall
At the East of the old school house
Heeding not our teacher's call
Oh, but time has wrought its changes
Like a vision is the past
And though hills and rocks divide us
We will meet them all at last

—*Ella MacKinnon Gammon,*
West Branch River John, Nova Scotia

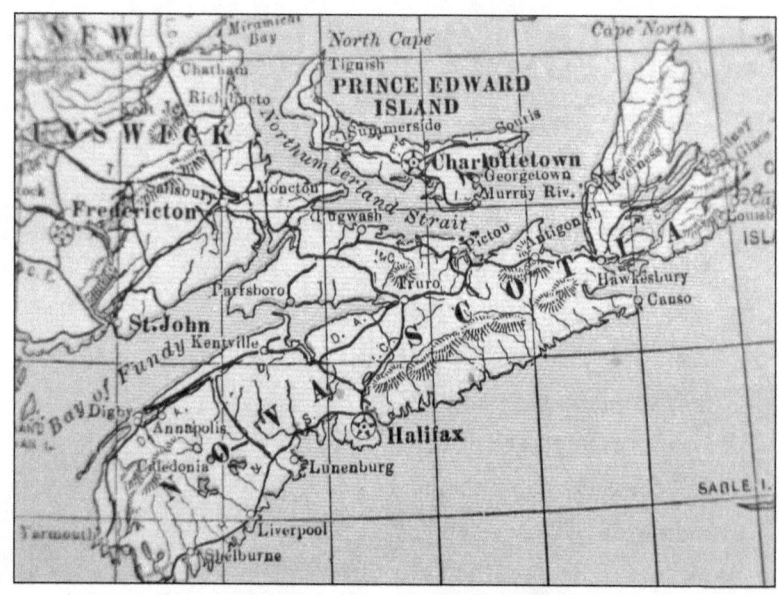

River John near Pictou on the Northumberland Strait

...you have become a great people, whilst we have melted away like snow beneath an April sun: our strength is wasted, our countless warriors dead, our forests laid low, you have hounded us from every place as with a wand, you have swept away all our pleasant land, and like some giant foe you tell us "willing or unwilling, you must go from amid these rocks and wastes.

—Little Pine, chief of the Garden River Ojibwe, from a letter to the governor of Canada, 1849

I cannot cross the great Lake to talk to you for my Canoe is too small, and I am old and weak. You cannot hear my voice across the Great Waters. I therefore send this Wampum and Paper talk to tell the Queen I am in trouble. My people are in trouble...No Hunting Grounds—No Beaver—No Otter—poor for ever...All these Woods once ours. Our Fathers possessed them all...White Man has taken all that was ours. Our Fathers possessed them all...White Man has taken all that was ours...Let us not perish.

—Chief Paussamigh Pemmeenaweet, a Petition to the Colonial office, Jan. 25, 1841

To Run Narrow

I am running. I am running for my life.

As I run I caution myself: *To run well you must first know the taste of blood. You must seal your lips with its thickness. You must run silent as a bird flies. Your sight must jump ahead of you as you outrun your enemy. Your enemy is somewhere behind you.*

The Mohawks are fierce but you must be fiercer.

Be firm as you run. Run narrower and narrower so that you go as one unseen. The tree branches are your brothers. They hide you in their leaves. You are running to save your life. Air whistles off your body. It streams down your back. Your ears ring. Sweat drips into your eyes, stings them.

Your feet barely touch the earth as you run. There is fire in your feet. Your bones feel hollow like the birds, your body buoyed by the wind. Caijebouguac, lonely river, is not far. The white settlers call it River John, but your people know it by its rightful name.

If you make it to the bay you will be close to safety. You will lay tight to the earth in the eelgrass and when the moment is right you will spring for your canoe. You will ask Grandfather to hold down your breath so no sound is carried off in the wind.

You will wait for high tide to separate you from your enemy.

Sew your lips with a needle-bone. Spread red stripes across your face. Make sure your knife parts a man's hair. Season the blade with Grandfather's chants, with the blessings of the sacred bear, and with the stoneknown for sharpening knives. Thank the stone for its firmness, for how it saves your life again and again.

*You are Stands Like a Tree. You are firm as an oak inside yourself.
You are the name given to you by your father, Lone Cloud, as you were
torn by the settlers from the arms of your mother.*

Lying in the eelgrass, you recall the one named Ella.

ELLA

I am Ella, born to West Branch River John, Pictou County, Nova Scotia. I am writing this to taste life twice; once in the inevitability of the moment, then again in tea-sipping solitude. I live so far away from civilization I sometimes feel like a tree's shadow. West Branch, part of River John, is tiny; we have but a dozen families in dwelling.

When my sisters and I chase butterflies in the graveyard next door my heart flies. It darts between stones that hold engraved names like *Anna Parsons O'Donnell, Wife of Jacob O'Donnell, William, Son of Hiram and Maude O'Grady, Lizabeth and twin, Tissie, Daughters of Emmel and Greta Hiller*—all tucked underneath their quilt of green.

But I do not want ever to die, to be put to the earth like a ground mole. If I fly down the hill fast enough with my arms above my head, I can outrace God's eye. If he does not notice me he will never call on me. That is just fine with myself. Invisible. I am invisible.

To remain invisible you cannot eat much. I never scoop for second helpings of haggis made with sheep's pluck, tatties, partridge stew, or venison, and I never partake of dessert. I command myself. *Ella*, I say, *you do not want to invite an early departure. You, my fine girl, want to live forever.* So it is with that conviction that I am captain of my own ship.

Ships are something we have plenty of too, especially in River John where ships are built, the continual chirr of saws spill into town, sawdust, like snow, covering pathways. Many of my friends' fathers work for the ship builders, and they make schooners, sloops and brigs that easily slide off log rounds set down to the water's edge.

I love the majestic sight when the boats are set afloat. They are the lovely wooden birds of the sea, their magnificent sails flapping like seagull wings in the wind. Sometimes a clergyman christens them and all the villagers gather to watch the ships set sail. It is a momentous undertaking. They bless the boats with sacred words and pray for their safety at sea.

We, my family and I, are Presbyterians. The Highland chiefs of Scotland drove out my ancestors when they drained families of land and cast them aside. Father, with his good fortune, left Scotland early on and was given a land grant, crown land in fact, in West Branch, Nova Scotia in 1825. He has lovingly worked his property ever since and cleared a pasture for our sheep and cattle.

Because of the Great Hunger from the potato famine, my father, at age sixteen, boarded a vessel named the Pigeon. Since only a few passengers could board the small ship, they were saved from outbreaks of small-pox and dysentery. Many another vessel has been quarantined for great lengths of time on the beaches of River John to stave off spreading such sickness. "Sickers' boats" we call them and stay clear of those passengers, their flesh white as suet, their clothes soiled. Should we pass such a person on the street, Mother has instructed we are to hold our breath lest we catch what ails them. She is not being disrespectful through such warning because she is concerned that one of her three daughters could fall ill to small-pox.

LIKE BIRDS TO A WINDOW

Before I forget, let me tell you this true story. When settlers first came to this province and the Micmac people searched for new hunting grounds, a woman went into the wilderness. She heard from several men, who regarded her a spinster, that there were sugar trees in Canada. Not knowing said sugar must be extracted with a spigot pounded into the maples, she pulled bark from the tree and put a chunk in her mouth and chewed and sucked. She returned to the village disgruntled and spit bark pieces from her mouth, nearly gagging on its bitterness. "You devilish men," she screamed, "You have made a right fool of me." After that she took to her room, barely leaving the village's log cabin where several families were housed.

Their laughter remained with her unto the day of her death—it was written in church logs that she cursed those men with her last breath. Her departure was the day of my birth. I was named after her because my mother, so loved the name Ella. My grandmother was closely acquainted with her family and she sometimes called me her Bella Ella. Ever since Mother has referred to me, upon occasions, with that very name which sends love, sweet as maple syrup, straight to my heart. It is only when I have been on my best behavior, though, that Bella Ella is ever uttered in our household.

I liked the way that nickname rhymed and I guess that sound joined me and filled my head with verses. Mother says, *You are a regular songstress,* and Father shrugs when he hears such words. Mother once snuck me a leather bound book of Robert Burn's poetry that I hid underneath my mattress because there is a poem in it called "A

Fond Kiss." Father would not approve. She does not want Father to catch me with such a book. He would say my head is given to demons. Sometimes even I think he might be right.

Voices come to me like spring birds to the window. I sit on my quilt, after my sisters have left the room, and listen to my head. I am entertained for hours in such a manner. Sometimes Robert Burns himself, the greatest Scot ever, speaks directly to me even though he died before my birth: "A fond kiss, and then we sever; A farewell, and then forever!" When sunshine laps at the window I feel Robbie's arms surround me. I think I am in love with him. I am, myself surely, his red, red rose. Because of this I am commanded to write my own poems. Perhaps one day I'll become a poet.

I imagine my life as an unborn, as pure spirit.

Because there are poetic thoughts roaming my head do not consider my life idle or removed from danger. There is danger not even my parents know of. One danger time happened a year back near the fenced-in ice skating rink in River John. Months afterwards a far worse danger arrived when Mother became sick. Sickness arrived and settled in like an unwanted relative.

No one must ever know of the skating rink episode. Several friends have been sworn to secrecy because they were there and partook of our shenanigans. We completed a laying on of hands over the Bible and vowed, most seriously and with earnest hearts, that none of us would speak of that mysterious evening. My parents would tether me to a chair if they knew; forbid me to attend further socials. Mind you, I went as one invisible, but I was not invisible when asking for permission.

"BILLY O'FLANNIGAN, YOU MUST remember him, Mother, from our prayer group, asked me to be his partner at the skate dance."

"Yes, Ella, I do remember him. He is quite a charmer."

Was there a slight rise of Mother's eyebrow? No, it must have been a nervous twitch. She is sometimes given to twitches and I tell her that I can see her nerves dancing on her face which always makes her laugh and she quickly covers her cheeks with her hands.

"There are going to be fiddlers from Halifax. You know how much I like fiddle music. May I go, Mother, oh please?" I tapped my feet on the floor while I waited for her reply as she swept the floor where earlier she spilled flour.

"Cassie mentioned you might ask so I have already talked with your father and he says yes, providing you mind your ways." I could feel the weight of her eyes on me after she gave me permission. It was as though she measured her decision and then questioned it. I supposed most parents carefully weighed what was wise for their children.

Readying for the Skate Dance

"Do not wiggle to and fro as I fit this dress to you," Mother says as she sticks pins into the hem. But I am humming out of sheer happiness and when one hums the body follows like an obedient servant, although I do manage to hold still long enough for her to stitch it up because it is my very best dress, the one with the puffy sleeves.

It seems Mother is continually letting hems out for me and my sisters. I do, as eldest daughter, sometimes wonder if having children is worth the effort, especially when daily life requires great stamina.

My sisters, Abbey and Cassie, and I are at the sprouting age. I even have growing pains. Father calls them stretch-you-on-the-rack pains. He tells me God wants humans to experience pain so they will contemplate holiness more often. I tell him I do not believe God knows of my presence on earth, therefore I am exempt. That is when he says, "You, daughter, have a contrary nature." He laughs and curls his upper lip, his beard obscuring his full mouth. There is a smutty smell to his beard from the pipe he smokes each evening after dinner. He is a blacksmith and I suppose because he forges hot iron all day, he has to keep some remnant of a fire going. It must warm him for the next day's work.

BILLY WAS TO FETCH ME IN West Branch via his family's sleigh but the hours dimmed into dusk with no sight of Billy anywhere. I fretted much, paced the floor until Mother said, "Sit, young lady. You are wearing a hole in the rug."

Mother, of course, was to accompany us. No fourteen year-old is allowed to attend socials without a proper chaperone. I am dressed in my red pretty, a gold sash tied at my waist, my hair freshly washed in melted snow and tied back in a matching gold ribbon. Mother, who still dons the traditional Highland plaid, a blanket, really, looked much like my bed mattress. All the same, I was pleased she would attend me. "*Be grateful,child*," she often reminds me. And I am.

Most clothes in Pictou County are made of linen and wool—the mainstays, and I feel fortunate to have one dress that is not a formless shift and that does not cause me endless itching. I have not, for the life of me, understood why the whiskers on wool cannot be shaved off and the material made smooth.

In our household, my sisters and I spin wool, sew and cook, milk the cows and work in the garden. My favorite garden work is planting potatoes in round hollows, four to five inches deep. Kennebec potatoes are the largest and my family prefers them. We labor long and spread horse manure around fresh plantings. We even removed ornery stones from the land so our mother could plant a flower garden beside our house.

There is much purpose to our daily lives and such work is comfort because it, in turn, makes comfort. Nothing is more satisfying than by the end of day, tired unto one's bones and finished with good work, to relax in the comfort of our own making.

AFTER SUPPER, WORD CAME BY free rider that Billy's sleigh hit a rock and that he and his father hauled the broken sleigh to their work shed. Would I meet him in River John? This caused much disturbance with Father and after we recited scripture, Father wrestled his hands to the point I thought he might twist off a finger.

With the passage of much silence, much seeming contemplation, he volunteered to harness our horses and take me into town. He ordered me to pick up the supper table and lay dry the dishes—which I promptly accomplished. Since it had become dark outside, Mother would now remain behind to attend my sisters' well-being. Perhaps it was such a change in plans that made trouble clench its fist and strike out. But whatever it was, the danger time lay in wait.

FATHER, WHENEVER IN TOWN, was given to much chatter with his brethren and they would eventually take up their pipes or snuff boxes in the enclosed building off the rink. It was not a watchful eye Father employed, but he was scrupulous in every other manner, especially when it came to his study of scripture. *"I study the divine to become divine,"* he has often said to me and my sisters, hoping those very words catch in our hearts.

But, alas, I am skeptical of God and have many questions, the most important one being: Why does God give us life only to renege on such a gift and take it back? Needless to say, I am greatly disillusioned. Yet, I mention no doubting matters to my parents. They would be chagrined by my questioning the sanctity of their long held beliefs.

With wool blankets wrapped around us, we took off over the moon spattered snow, the horse bells more splendid than I previously recalled. Perhaps the cold itself let the bells ring in a more melodious tone. The air that night felt as though it held spoken words—I could nearly see them mid-air, frozen in place like crystal stars.

Oh joyful, joyful night! Joyful trees that make shadows come to life and dance upon the earth in winter; the sweeping, simple majesty of earthly things. I sang this several times out loud on the way to town and Father said: "I believe there might be a poet inside you."

I have determined one cannot hold in such beauty because it is a wondrous land I live upon. A land filled with animals, birds and many varieties of wildflowers. In summer the fields sway like waves from the sea. Yet it is the sea I fear most and sometimes have the night terrors—myself sinking into water's murderous depths. Fear is tucked far back in my mind. The murky dark, as seen from father's fishing boat, seems endlessly thick.

As we drew near the rink my friends called out "Ella, Ella," and we were greeted with such boisterous cheer I felt myself blush. With caution, lest my petticoat get caught on the sideboard, Father lowered me onto the snowy ground, my wool socks chafing my ankles. The air smelled of vanilla.

Gliding on Ice

There were burn barrels set out on the ice rink to warm skaters and the fence was decorated in pine and cedar boughs, threaded with red berry sprigs. I thought how fortunate we were to have such a rink.

"Let me carry those for you," Billy offered as he took my ice skates. I followed him to the wooden benches lining one side of the rink and we sat down to pull on our ice-skates. Mine had red and white candy-cane laces from last year's Christmas which dressed up their scuffed leather. The look of the skates caused me some embarrassment, but my family could not afford new ones. I tucked, far back underneath the bench, my sturdy brown leather lace-ups that served me for both winter and summer. Shoes are of great importance in cold country. There have been those who lost toes or an entire foot for lack of good footwear.

My family cautioned me to mind my feet in the cold. Frostbite could lead to gangrene. The black scourge we young ones call it, as old man Carlson from Toney River learned. It was his unfortunate fate to have no boots. With just socks and shoddy shoes, their soles worn through, Old Carlson plowed on-foot through mounds of snow to reach River John for supplies, his wife Betsey bedridden and in need of sustenance. A week later, when foot trouble set in, a neighbor brought him back to town.

"Don't take my feet," he begged the doctor, but Doc Williams took them anyway. Six men held him down, he thrashing at the doctor. Word had it Doc Williams threw out his frock coat afterwards due to the amount of spattered blood. It pains me to think of Old Carson's agony—the poor man loaded up with whiskey to ease the pain that could not be eased. It was also said that Doc Williams imbibed a healthy amount of leftover whiskey, that he told those in attendance there was no task more difficult than to saw off a limb.

But I must not dwell on the difficulties of others.

The skate rink was filled with skaters. They spun carefree as angels. Billy wore a red scarf. The color accentuated his rosy cheeks. He had brown sideburns which gave him a wise countenance. He looked like a Christmas package waiting to be unwrapped. He was a good foot taller than I, his body sturdy as a fence post. He smelled of nutmeg. His every glance told me he was quite smitten but that was unwise on his part. Plans for my future could easily curtail any possibility with him. Who knows, I might become a poet or a doctor. I was especially interested in becoming a doctor after I heard about old Carson.

Skaters glide-danced. It was a practice borrowed from New England where they held skating championships, the results of which are published in The Tinder. None of us were champions, although we wished we were. It is most difficult to dance with skates on, but we modified movements to fit our needs. Millie and my best friend Ernestine were already on the ice, their hands around their beaus waists. They looked my way and smiled. Millie's braids whipped upward as she ducked underneath Colin's arm.

The fiddlers played "Welcome to Your Feet Again," and I so excitedly rose that I nearly spilled myself onto the rink; Billy grabbed my arm to steady me. Just as we neared the other skaters, Father appeared. He was dapper in his wool waistcoat and breeches. "I will be in the room off the rink," he said, merriment in his eyes. "Do not break an ankle," he warned and reached for his snuff box. *High Dry Toast* is his favorite and Mother bought him two cans from a tobacconist's shop in Halifax. He uses it only on the rarest occasions, says the Almighty would disapprove of excess. "Give me your hand," Billy whispered as he guided me to the center of the rink. His hand was warm as bread from the oven. Father stood back underneath a rafter and watched us before finally stepping into the side room. He winked and disappeared.

My skates blazed across the rink. I imagined little flickers of ice crystals rising underfoot. We glided around the burn barrels, wood smoke filled my nose and made me sneeze. Classmates watched as we ducked underneath each other's arms. The air filled with fiddles and laughter. Billy fell behind and whistled me to slow down.

"Ella, why do you always have to be in the lead?" but I paid him no attention. The rink whizzed by in a collage of colors; decorations on the wall became a blur. Billy caught up and swirled me around, his breath soft against my cheek.

"My honey bee," he called me.

"Why call me that name?"

"Because you are sweet as honey, or nearly so."

"Why only nearly?"

"Why so many questions?" and he broke into a smile that revealed his lovely dimples. Dimples are charming on a young man. They show a certain sense of humor. They must be storage chests of goodness. Perhaps good cheer is magical. If so, my sister Abbey could use some.

As we drank warm milk and ate biscuits and cookies, Ernestine, Millie, their dance partners Colin and John joined us. They were breathless and had a feverish anxiety about them. Ernestine was fairly bursting with something she knew that I did not. She got this puffed partridge look whenever she knew something ahead of me and it most irritated me.

"We hear there is a party on the bay. Want to join us?" Colin inquired.

"What kind?" Billy asked and added, "There had better be no illegal alcohol down there."

A knot grew in my stomach at the thought of leaving the rink. What would Mother and Father think if they were to find out? Not once had I disobeyed their instructions. I twisted my dress between my fingers.

"Come on, join us," Colin urged, his hands danced in excitement, a brazen dare set in his sky-blue eyes. He slung his arm over Millie's shoulder. Millie looked like a rumpled tea towel from attempting to outdo him on the rink and the ribbons on her braids had come undone and hung like limp banners.

"It is not far. Just down the hill."

My throat tightened and my heart skipped. "But I have never set a foot on bay ice and am most fearful of underneath things." They paid no attention.

I imagined shoals of fish, straggly seaweed hair and strange creatures that lurked about. The breaking up of ice beneath my very feet was not an experience I would court; my body hurtling toward some frightful destination where black grows so deep one becomes sightless. The thought of the cold dark world froze me to one spot. My temples throbbed. I had once fallen from Father's boat and my fear was real.

"Hurry up. There is little time left us," Colin urged.

"Will you come?" Billy asked as he tugged on my arm. "We will be gone but a wink's time and we will be back before you know it."

It was with a heavy heart that I slipped off my skates and tied my brown leathers. All the while my breath like a stubborn mule. "Take my hand," I asked Billy as we moved past the eyes of the unsuspecting.

The six of us ran down the hill toward the bay—moonlight set the snow ablaze. Snow crunched underneath us and the wind whistled mournfully through the branches. The cold surged through my mittens.

Colin and Millie giggled with excitement. I doubted her parents would approve our actions. They were most devout and belonged to the Church of Scotland. No, they would severely punish her if they suspected such antics. Millie told me she was once sentenced to her room without supper or morning porridge for sassing her mother. Chores around her house were multiplied for an entire month and often Millie complained of the excessive work.

With certitude, I feared we were nearing danger and that once that line was crossed there was no turning back. Perhaps trouble became a multiplying factor. I ran my mitten across my cheek, up and over my brow as though to rearrange my thoughts. Oh, now I am damned for sure and will be cast amongst the heathens on Judgment Day.

I thought of Mother and my sisters by the fire knitting socks and mittens. I longed for warm tea, the orderliness that runs our family.

Hopefully, Father had not broken from his friends to check on me. He would be so very startled to find me missing and I greatly feared the consequences of my actions. Father is a gentle man, but once riled he becomes gruff as an old bear.

Colin was the first to step onto the ice. His lantern swung back and forth as he beckoned us forward. John, the ship builder's son, was right behind him. Both inched ahead to test the ice. If the ice started to crack they could become moored on a sheet of it. Many an unsuspecting person floated out to sea on a sheet of ice that broke into a floating island. I could almost see the water lapping up over the surface of the breakaway ice and again my breath caught in my chest. I imagined my ribs as a ladder for breath; that my rib-bones too were slippery with fear.

Ernestine yelled she wanted to head up hill and back to the rink. John yelled, "Go ahead, silly girl."

She spat back to him that she was no silly girl and that he best take his words and apply them to himself. But, in reality, she was afraid to climb up the hill alone. She stood still for a moment, both hands on her hips, her muslin skirt flapping like a bird struck with a sling-shot.

STANDS LIKE A TREE SPEAKS

That night the young ones came down onto the frozen bay was a time I would not soon forget. I bored a large hole in the ice and it took much labor, the gun which originally belonged to Father rested on a snow bank beside me. But I was not out to ice fish on this night.

Not long after the hole was made, I saw the young ones run down towards me. I crouched low to the ice, watched as they flitted about, young birds on a dangerous flight. A girl cried out, the one they called Ella, "I cannot set foot upon the ice," but the boys begged her to do so. "Come on Ella. We will watch out for you."

"I am afraid," she yelled back.

I recognized the name Ella from when I was at her father's forging shop, a man of stout heart, Ebenezer. I worked his fence line, replaced broken posts, and he, in exchange, hammered out new iron runners for my sled. The new runners were faster than the wooden ones our people depended on. Ella, that day, came into her father's shop, his noon-meal in her hands, and she startled momentarily. Her father introduced her to me. I keenly remember the part of her hair, her earnest blue eyes, but mostly it was her voice that impressed me—a voice so close to song it was like brook water as it ripples over stones. I do not know why, but that voice remained with me.

Somewhere in the distance an owl hooted and for a moment the frolicking youngsters grew silent; the windows of the skate rink on the hill flickered with lanterns and the building itself seemed to have eyes to watch out on the evening's events.

Should I go? Leave them to themselves? What of the bored hole? Could a child trip and get hurt?

With only my father's girdle for wear and a deer hide over my shoulders, I bitterly felt the sting of the winter's night; my moose skin moccasins inadequate. I wrapped my leggings tighter and tied them off.

There is the cold and the cold that eats into the cold, but nothing was colder than my removal from my family when I was six-years of age. The family that took me in and to prevent my escaping they told me how many in my own family were reduced to begging in River John and nearby towns. Their clothes, if they were fortunate enough to have any, were worn to shreds. This cold I could certainly withstand.

Just before removal from my natural family, Father whispered, `"*You shall be known as Stands Like a Tree*," and somehow that name suited me and I reclaimed it when finally free from those that housed me. But not before the pious one and his Mrs. sent me to their school for a "proper" education, as well as instruction of their religion.

No longer do I wear the White Man's hair—mine now cropped close in front, long in back.

"There is no party here," a girl said.

Someone replied, "Finnegan said meet me on the ice below the skate rink."

"He was fooling you," another added. "He was just up to his old tricks. Remember how he told us there was a fire at the schoolhouse and we all secretly wished that building with its wretched drafts would catch? It was a fib."

"Let us head back," a girl uttered.

But there I was with a white man's gun. There would be no sufficient explaining. If I were to run off they would call for help. The cold bit into me like a starved dog. My feet grew stiff.

Let me explain how I came by the gun.

FATHER, THINKING I WOULD have assumed the settlers' ways, kept his distance from me. For years we never spoke. In the village a merchant mentioned seeing my father's encampment. Since Father was Chief Lone Cloud, there was a close accounting of his where-abouts. I listened intently so as to follow the foot path of the fur merchant's words and committed to memory the exact hill near Tatamagouche upon which Father was said to have staked his encampment.

"Father, Father," I called out as I neared the wigwam where he was believed to be, but no answer arose. Would he recognize me after all these years? With cautious footsteps I approached his entryway, pulled back the birch bark door, but the inside of his shelter was empty, the girdle he once wore the only remnant that remained—as well as a gun. Where had it come from? How had he come by it? Father said, when I was but a youngster, that to own a white man's gun was to own his crime. It was unlikely a white man gave him such a weapon.

There was an eerie silence in the wigwam, nearby shelters as si-lent as my father's. Had my people fled? I turned away but not be-fore fetching my father's things. It seemed the Great Spirit of all my Peoples begged me to take leave and upon my leave-taking I did not look back. Hundreds of spirits seemed to push me in order to re-move me from that encampment.

THE YOUNG PEOPLE WERE closing in. If I scared them they might become more cautious of stepping further onto the ice. With that made clear to myself, I stood against the billowing wind. Screams rose when the youngsters saw me. I picked up the gun with my right hand and brandished the weapon towards the seven directions of my world.

The youngsters did not move. They were stilled like startled deer.

"If we turn and run, he will shoot us," one of them cried.

I raved with the gun in my hand. My ancestral chant beat against my chest and in moving to and fro my body's heat rose higher and higher. I whirled in the air and my ancestors whirled with me. No longer cold. And no longer did I see those youngsters who just sec-onds earlier screamed. The power of my people stirred within me and I recalled something from childhood before the settlers took me from them. Grandfather and Grandmother, both long dead, grew clear in my vision as they witnessed me in our old ways at the Walking-Out Ceremony; Stands Like a Tree on his very first snowshoes as he was introduced by his people to the forest.

Five-year old Stands Like a Tree, after the ceremony, could begin to walk with his people without becoming an undue burden as they traveled from fishing shores to winter lodging. My father, Lone Cloud, was beside me, proud that his son could step forth on his own.

The ice hole became a fire pit and from it spirits rose, some I knew, others were a mystery, but all were of Micmac, First Nation ancestry. There in the swirling of upward bound spirits an eagle soared. I was no longer made of flesh and blood. I was bone of tree and breath of wind and heart of stone. No longer bound by my body, I became a soaring spirit. From above, as on a branch, I saw the frightened, wide-eyed children, and in particular, I saw the one called Ella.

ELLA TELLS OF THAT NIGHT

There he was before us, dancing in godforsaken abandonment. I could not unbind my fears, my great shock, but neither could I turn away my eyes. "Billy, let us flee," I pleaded. But no, he would not turn back on a raving man with a gun any more than I could turn away, entrapped by my dumbstruck gaze.

Billy hollered, "What are you doing here? This is our bay." He shoved his hat to the back of his head, attempting more authority. "Do you hear me, heathen? This is our bay. The ship builders own it. Get the blazes back to the woods where you belong." Billy took a few steps forward, his shoulders looking wider, more muscular.

Never before had I seen this side of Billy. I always thought him a compassionate young man and not someone who would claim the bay solely his, or yell such outrageous insult. The Micmac families, as Father said, were not wild and they were certainly not heathens, but I could not be absolutely certain he was Micmac. If he was Mohawk we certainly were in trouble.

"Stop it. Stop such nonsense," I yelled. Anger rose in the pit of my stomach. I imagined animals running wild in my belly.

Moonlight turned the man's skin the purest gold and his hair was tinted birch bark white. His chanting took on the shape of animals and in his words I saw coyote, moose and deer. In a magnificent cape, animals swirled around him. His eyes held a strange glint whenever he cast a glance our way.

Without warning, Ernestine broke from the group and fled up the hill, her scarf falling behind her. Millie tugged at my coat, begged me follow. I was fearful, yet still captivated and held my ground. I had not, as yet, recognized the man.

Millie shook her finger underneath my nose and said, "You stubborn girl." She turned, fairly shoved by fright, and sped uphill behind Ernestine, hollering at her friend to wait up. She scooped down to fetch the scarf Ernestine dropped.

"Ella, come now," she turned and pleaded, a quiver in her voice, but I was not swayed.

Then, in real fear, I warned her, "Tell Ernestine to say nothing of this. If she does she will miss more than her supper and porridge."

I turned back upon the dancing man. His arm rose to the sky as though he were brandishing a spear. His words were heavy as clouds. But there was no way for me to discern his true meaning. He somehow seemed familiar.

Both Colin and John remained crouched to the ground, at considerable distance, as though the earth's dark blanket might somehow protect them, as though they could not be seen in the shadowy night. They groaned under fear.

"What in God's name is he doing?" John asked.

"Practicing strangeness is what I think," Colin replied and then pulled his coon-cap down over his ears.

Billy, on his stomach, wiggled his way closer and leaned forward on his elbows to better see. I crept toward Billy to keep him from doing something irrational.

This man in his simple girdle and animal skin changed from fearful to reverent, or perhaps my eyes had begun to register him differently as he grew lost to his chant. There was now a reverence in his voice never before heard by myself in even our best prayer meetings.

It seemed there were rivers in his voice, the wind, the ocean as it pounded on shore and the cascading rain. Words slipped through his mouth in a near magical way. We were watching something sacred, of that there was certainty. Billy, all the while, continued behaving in the most annoying manner, calling out repugnant names.

The man bent and pushed the gun into a snow bank, barrel first.

Another thought entered my head. What if Father were to find me here transfixed? Worry grew inside me, and I whispered to Billy, "Let us turn back."

Billy said, "Hush, Ella. Bite your tongue. Have you lost your mind?"

He crawled ever closer to the man.

"What are you doing?" I asked. He did not reply. Billy looked much like the raccoons that plagued our supply shed. One year they broke into our shed and ate all the feed for the sheep. Father cursed them and grew so angry his skin nearly burst into flame. That is when I learned Father's limits. He would take so much trouble but there would come a moment where he would break into a rage. I had only seen this once and did not want to see it again, especially on account of me.

Again, Billy hollered at him, but to no avail.

The man ceased dancing. He recited a chant, this time in English. It seemed a chant of empowerment. There were owls; the largest ever seen in these parts, flying above Colin, Billy, John and me. They blocked out the moon. There was no way to explain the mystery of this and there was no certainty the others saw what I saw.

The man called spirits to flock over the bay. That is when I realized that I, too, stood on the frozen bay, currents of water churning in madness beneath my feet. I prayed the ice hold, that I not tumble into its frigid depths. Surely I would lose all track of myself in such a watery world. I imagined the fish and eels flitting about. It was mostly the eels that troubled me. They were the ugliest creatures of the water world, their sinuous bodies slicked in slime.

Soon, only silence. The man bent and picked up the gun. He pulled his deer hide over his shoulder. I held my breath as he uttered a very low chant. He ran his hand up and down the barrel of the gun and repeated something. Then he stood in concentration for a moment before ramming the gun down the hole in the ice.

To considerable shock, the man called out my name. "Ella, come here." He must also have heard my name when Billy yelled at me. With trepidation, I did as he bid and walked toward him and wondered how he knew my name. It was then that I recalled his visit to Father's shop and how Father had said, "Ella, extend your hand to my Micmac friend."

"Idiot," Billy called after me. "I am going back to the rink."

I yelled, "Go ahead!"

Something grew sturdy inside me.—perhaps the very ice I stood on firmed my bones. There was I, a young woman, standing next to the tall Micmac who must have been four years older than Billy, a man really. He smelled of wilderness, of the forest in spring when things are moist upon the sweetgrass.

"Come back here," Billy called as he headed uphill. "Get away from him, Ella!"

I paid him no heed. Some compulsion, I knew not what, pushed me forward. I extended my hand to the man. He reached into a small deerskin sack that hung around his neck and pulled out a small beaded object. Into my hand he pressed a most lovely beaded eight point star and simply said, "You, my child, have been touched by the stars." The meaning of his words made no sense to me.

"Why do you say this?"

"I tell you this to give you power for what is ahead. I tell you this because of the spirits I heard in your voice. Treasure your voice. It is a gift."

He turned me toward my remaining friends and said, "I buried the gun deep in the water to rid my people of the misery guns have wrought upon our land. Should you ever need me, I am known as Stands Like a Tree. You can sometimes find me at the Widow Minnie's house."

"Go now," he said, giving my shoulder a light push.

For a moment my feet would not move. I was spellbound, weighted with a mystery too deep for my comprehension. So badly I wanted to turn around, throw my arms around the one who bestowed such a gift. I would now have two items that must remain hidden from Father—this lovely beadwork and the book of poems by my Scottish hero.

"Let us hurry back," Colin said.

Anxious to return lest Father find me missing, I sped up the hill behind the others. I turned to wave to the man, but he had disappeared. The owls, too, were gone and the moon had returned in its fullness.

"Say nothing of this evening to your parents," Colin urged. "We will warn Ernestine and Millie, too."

"After school we will hold a ceremony to silence," I added.

To this they agreed and quizzed me why I spoke to the man. But I said nothing. Even I did not understand my reasons. Afterwards, there was a great cooling off of my affection for Billy. He had spat on the ground near the Micmac with such vehemence.

And so it was, Father and I rode home as though nothing unusual impressed itself upon the evening. He was jovial and animated as he told me about Rev. John Clark Benton, who once attended the London Missionary Society and spent many a sick day as he sailed home to River John. The poor man nearly threw himself overboard from constant retching. Not even the ship's cook found remedy to soothe the poor Reverend's stomach.

"The very waves reached inside him and rubbed his innards with grains of salt," and as Father retold the Reverend's words and difficult sea passage he slapped his leg with his hand, his laughter so fierce I thought he would spill from the sleigh. "I know it is not funny to laugh at another man's trouble, Ella," he said, "But that man's bragged for years about his great courage and stamina under difficulty. I would not have such a reaction were it anyone else."

He reached over and patted the back of my hand and added, "Say nothing to Mother of the Reverend's sea passage. She would not take kindly to my amusement on his account."

I did not say a thing. My love for my father was one filled with awe and I felt great shame for leaving the rink the minute he joined his friends. My secret burned in my chest and I supposed that very burning was righteous payback for fibbing.

But Father laughed little after that trip to town—Mother soon took sick and much changed in our lives. Sorrow spread its wings over our household and darkness spread like a shadow over all we had known.

House Made of Grief

"It is cancer," Doc Williams told Father. "Big as a fist in her stomach. The cancer has probably been there for some time, judging from the size of it. They start out tiny and multiply quicker than the wink of an eye."

Father knocked his knuckles over the kitchen tabletop, his brow knitted in worry.

"Tell me different," he said. "Give me at least a sliver's worth of hope."

"I wish that was possible," said the kindly doctor as he began to pace. "I have seen this kind of cancer before. There is no remedy in all God's land. All we can do is offer comfort, turn pillows, change sheets and pray. Teas might help for pain and I have some *Soothing Calm* made from red clover and mixed with honey."

"How long does she have?" Doc Williams only shook his head and mumbled nothing understandable.

Father, for the first time, seemed as a lost child, his knuckles knocking on wood. He pulled at his beard. Even though he appeared woeful like a child there was an adult's heaviness to his countenance that made his face unusually old. I feared for my sisters, I feared for myself and mostly I feared for my father.

It was my mother who gave order and cheer to the house. It was my mother who helped us believe gold lined our hearts with goodness. It was my mother's songs I carried in my breast, songs her mother taught her and that came from Scotland. I loved the mystery, the rhyme, the cadence of the sometimes mournful ballads. And Mother's voice was husky, not a common feminine voice built on the edge of emotion. Whenever we traveled to the village to fetch supplies, men would turn their heads the moment she opened her mouth. Sometimes they would even ask her to repeat herself in order to hear her voice again.

Oh goodness, what would we do without her presence? Without her firm cheer?

Father walked the doctor to the door. He took the bottle of *Soothing Calm,* set it on a shelf, and asked how he should administer it.

"Only if she complains of pain," said Doc Williams, "and only two teaspoons every six hours. If it makes her throw-up, give her but one teaspoon every six hours."

Then he hugged my father, his white hair splashed over his vest, his spectacles halfway down on the bridge of his nose. For a moment, I thought he was holding Father up, that Father's legs would buckle under such weighty news. He seemed small in the even smaller man's arms.

"Send a rider in if you need me. You are a good man. I would get up at any hour to attend your fine family. You must surely know that, Ebenezer."

Upon closing the heavy wood door, father leaned into it and buried his head in his arms and sobbed such sadness as was never before witnessed in our household. My throat clogged with my own tears. I stood at the hearth, myself in need of warmth. I thought back on the times I saw Mother clasp herself around the stomach and thought then she was only gathering her wits about her, that the chores she attended were taking a toll. But no, it was far more serious.

"Go to your room, Ella. I must be alone. Pray, child. Pray."

From behind my closed door I heard his tears speak. They told of his love for my mother. They told how they met one day in March at a sugaring festival, a family story often recounted to my sisters and me. Not until the following year had he built enough courage to ask her hand in marriage.

Father, to this day, remains a shy man. For all his good looks, his fine physical prowess, he becomes reticent in crowds and draws to the nearest corner. It is Mother who speaks for him, who knows the right words for the villagers and who sets up all social engagements. It is she who charms strangers with her warmth. It is she who carries baskets of food into the village for mourners and those stricken with sickness.

I heard my parents talking in their bedroom. A little later, as I pumped myself some water from the hand pump by the sink, he fetched her tea and crumpets spread with thick butter, a hardboiled egg preserved in lime-water, and blackberry jam. She had asked for a small repast, and he, faithful to her need, always complied. I kept the door ajar. Perhaps it was not true, the report of cancer. Doc Williams was known to be off the mark a few times. I got myself a hardboiled egg from the crockery pot and slipped back into my sisters' and my bedroom.

There was I, a fourteen year-old girl sitting in the middle of her bed nibbling a design around the egg's white belly. I cared not to read Robert Burns nor could I muster a prayer. All there was in that room became cold and dark. Sadness will churn out its own weather, of that I was certain. It can freeze a room and all its occupants. I was most grateful that my younger sisters Abbey and Cassie were staying with Aunt Kathleen in Tatamagouche. She is Mother's sister and they are the best of friends.

But already the world seemed far lonelier and more frightful than ever before. I picked at the bed covers, rolled them down and crawled in. If I could not have the comfort of the hearth, I would have comfort from my quilts. Still, I shivered until my teeth chattered. The winter wind howled at the window and the house already had an unattended smell. It seemed as if even the furniture took up mourning. From the side table I fetched my writing slate and wrote with a stub of chalk:

CHILDHOOD'S HOPES

When a child at school how often
I Burns's poems did admire
And some day to be a poet
Was my only great desire.

That was all I could write. Worry consumed me. Had God made note of that night when I disobeyed Father? I certainly did not run back to the rink when Stands Like a Tree whirled in a fever of dance and chants. No, I was absorbed in watching him. Could it be Mother's sickness was sent to our household as punishment for that fateful night? Most certainly I deserved some chastisement. I have never easily tolerated deceitfulness, and now I was filled with it. It practically smothered me.

Why had it so bothered me when Ernestine told me about sneaking from the pantry at her home some coveted chocolate sent to her family from relatives in England? She was warned by her mother not to touch the chocolate. But why did that confession from her eat at me when I, too, went against my parents' caution? It is far too easy to believe one has not erred and to cover that wrong with all kinds of justifications.

Without supper or comfort from either parent I became lost to my room and to my mind. Never did I have such a restless night. I repeated spells to help heal my mother, spells Millie, Ernestine and I made up after we touched a wart-covered toad. I could not pray. That somehow felt unearned, and I was not sure a God even existed. I was someone who disobeyed parents by sneaking down onto the frozen bay. Hence, I deserved nothing.

In the restless current of dreams I managed to fall into slumber, my covers sullen comfort, my corn husk mattress crinkling each time I turned. My dreams scattered as fall leaves. Memory of them at dawn was impossible. I awakened to Father's knock on the door. He said, "Come, Ella, Mother wants to speak to you." He apologized for their taking to bed early without saying goodnight, and added he was numb from Doc Williams' diagnosis. "Please forgive my slight. You too must have much sadness."

Mother's face was the color of summer squash. Her white night-dress was buttoned tight under her neck. The side table held a half-eaten crumpet, crumbs and jam trailing the plate. She patted the bed and said, "Sit down beside me." The room held a scent of sickness like when a small lamb struggles and withers into death. It reminded me of Father's cattle shed, occasionally a shelter of death, sick animals now and then put down with his shotgun and hauled off later.

When Mother spoke her voice was dry, not the usual huskiness she was known for. I hollered to Father to put the kettle on. I wanted to soak her voice in tea. Mother ran her hand over the back of mine and I dared not move. Her touch was warm and my heart filled.

"Much will fall upon you, Ella. You are to help with your sisters and you must do extra chores around the house should I die."

"You are not going to die. You are too young. Doc Williams has been wrong before. Remember that man who walked all the way in winter from Toney River to River John to fetch his wife supplies? Well, the good Doctor said he would not live long hobbling around on those wooden pegs for legs. You are not going to believe this Mother, but I saw him in town just the other day and he looked fine. So the good doctor was wrong."

Mother's eyes became pools ready to overflow. She pulled me to her and I rested my head upon her chest. She stroked the full length of my hair. "I love you and Abbey and Cassie and your father with everything inside me. Be assured, I will fight this thing, but I cannot promise I will pull through. It is up to God. You know my fierce spirit, Ella. Any woman that chases a wolf away from the sheep field is capable of surmounting anything."

I sobbed great heaving sobs. I had kept so much inside me on account of Father, not wanting to increase his grief. Tears streamed into my mouth. All the while Mother cuddled me close. I hoped with all my heart that she would be with us for the holidays. Father inched his way into the room and carried a tray of eggs, bacon and specialty tea from London. On the tray was a dish for me. He sat in the stiff wooden chair beside the bed. "Eat up, Ella, before your breakfast goes cold." There were circles underneath his eyes.

The bacon's taste reminded me of salty tears. It tasted of sadness and the eggs slid down my throat like cod liver oil. Outside, a blizzard transformed the world into a ghostly white. With only one window in their bedroom, a small amount of light came into the room, revealing cobwebs along the wooden beams. Mother ate heartily and that gave me some comfort. I wiped the crumbs from the corners of her mouth, fetched a cloth and washed her face fresh. She smiled a smile big as the Hunter's Moon, my favorite fall sight.

With the tray in hand, I headed to the kitchen to begin those tasks now entrusted me. I opened the front door and heaped much snow into my pail to boil on the stove for dishes. The outside world breezed by in a cascade of the most brilliant snow I yet had the good fortune to see. From behind me I heard Father say, "Child, close that door. You are defeating the good will of our fire."

Comfort fell upon me. I could handle this. By steadfast work I would keep my Mother's death at bay. By doing tasks with all my heart, I would even erase my actions that night at the skate party. One could atone for one's sins. Of that I was certain. My days would now fill with the most earnest efforts.

I was a good girl, even though wrong once tempted me. It was curiosity that got the best of me. But now I set out to put things straight between my Maker and myself. And for some unexplainable reason Stands Like a Tree stood by me. In his face I saw the strength I now needed. And strength, unknown at the time, would be required in the days ahead.

CONTENDING WITH SISTERS

When Abbey slapped Cassie across the face all reasonableness left my being and jolted me off my chair where I had been consumed with knitting.

"By Jove, did you do that?" I yelled. Cassie's cheek had turned bright red, finger marks set in stripes alongside her face.

"She called me fat when I am lean as a winter's mouse," Abbey replied.

"She is lying. I did not call her any such thing. You know I never intentionally provoke Abbey."

Cassie ran to our bedroom and slammed the door. "Come on out," I called after her. Mother, from her sickbed asked what the hub-bub was all about.

"Just a quarrel," I said.

I pointed to the chair and ordered Abbey to sit and explain her-self. She sat cross-armed and stiff in self-righteousness. Her defiance set her lips tight and she spoke not a word, not a grumble. I grabbed her by the shoulders and shook her, demanding she speak. It was perhaps her silence that angered me more than her slapping Cassie.

"Cannot tell you," she finally responded and again barricaded her lips.

"You know Mother is not well. Why must you behave in such a manner?"

Abbey shook her head and let out a deep sigh, a sigh that indicat-ed *You bore me.* I called Cassie from our bedroom and asked that she explain what happened.

Cassie looked around the kitchen with a furtive eye, an eye that said she was afraid to speak. Without an ounce of compliance by either sister there was no choice but to heap chores upon both. Abbey would get the most difficult tasks.

"Abbey, you are to bring in wood, plus tidy up the privy, scrub its seat clean. When you are finished with those tasks you can shovel the walkway and lay down some dirt so when Father takes Mother into town to see Doc Williams she will not slip."

"Cassie, you will help me wash Mother's bedding, air the pillows."

Abbey let out a groan and announced, with a toss of her head, "I am telling Father when he returns from the shop. You always give Cassie the easiest chores. It is not fair."

"Life is not fair. Get used to it. You have much to pray about this Sunday and you best ask the Almighty for forgiveness. Just who do you think you are?" And with that said I began dusting the cobwebs from the kitchen rafters.

"I will start with the outhouse first just to get out of your way, Ella. You always favor Cassie and I am sick of it."

Abbey pulled on her coat, fetched some scrubbing rags and pumped some water. She banged the door closed making snow cascade off the roof and land with a thump.

"Good, some cold air might cool her off," I remarked once she was out of the house.

With Abbey in the outhouse and a good distance from Cassie, Cassie confided the reason for their quarrel. Abbey, without permission, had removed the buttons from Cassie's finest Sunday dress to sew upon her own best outfit. The buttons were shiny pearls, with a trim of delicate filigree that Father fashioned for Cassie's eleventh birthday.

"I am only borrowing them," Abbey told her. "I will remove them soon as church is over and sew them proper back onto your dress. You will never know anything was disturbed."

"But they were not yours to take in the first place and furthermore you never asked me. I was planning on wearing that very dress to church with my white pinafore," Cassie lamented.

"You can be certain she will promptly undo every button after the chores I gave her and sew them back onto your dress," I said." Let us get on with Mother's bedding. I have water on the stove for the sheets. Say nothing of this matter to either Father or Mother. They have worries enough and we must not rile them."

Cassie, still stunned by Abbey's audacious behavior, pouted, so to cheer her up, I said, "Tomorrow you get to help me make candles. In the morning lay out the mutton tallow, camphor, beeswax and two ounces of alum. You know what fun we have making candles. Abbey will clean up any mess, of that you can be certain. Perhaps we will even decorate a few candles. I think we still have some pressed wildflowers we can set into each candle."

Cassie smiled at this and hummed. Never did she look more content than when a tune filled her. Candle making was an art and something the family enjoyed, especially the ones for holiday gifts or birthdays.

A Visit to Father's Shop

Christmas was three weeks off but our house felt snowbound, stuck between action and inaction. Just as the pine boughs were heavily laden with snow, our hearts too were laden with worry. The trips into town to see Doc Williams or his visits to our household were coming more frequently. Mother's skin looked like colorless porridge and she ate little, though sipped soup now and then. We kept a large kettle of beef shank soup on the stove just in case she asked for nourishment. Beef seemed a sturdier soup for one so sick.

Not once during this time did I read the poems of Robert Burns. Poetry, as of late, seemed a frivolous activity. Nor could I concentrate on my studies. I hardly picked up my slate and chalk and missed many days of school while my younger sisters attended their lessons. Cassie brought home my schoolwork for the day, but more often than not I had no energy for it. Once in a while she carried a note from Ernestine who would inquire as to Mother's health or convey the latest news about classmates. But school was removed from my thoughts. If I worked hard enough, kept busy throughout the day, churned butter, fed the chickens and swept the house, I might just intervene with Mother's condition.

My favorite job was to clean out the cold chest underneath the kitchen floor. There was a trap door to first prop with a stick, and on my knees, I would pull out eggs, butter, meat, milk and even bread. We kept honey and syrup in the cold chest too so that bugs would not invade the house. Any sweetness left out of the chest became an open invitation to insects. They seemed to send messages off to their friends that said our kitchen was ripe for meals. Sometimes an insect would get stuck on one of the containers and we would squeal removing it, making quite the spectacle of ourselves.

The cold chest was six feet by three and lined with the most marvelous cedar; its scent filled the kitchen with a woody fragrance. But best of all, I liked taking inventory of what was on hand—it was creative to plan out the meals, run fixings for supper through my head. A small farm such as ours required much labor from each family member.

Father was extraordinarily busy or else he put extra work into his hands to keep from worry. I carried his meals out to his shop, watched as he hammered iron on an anvil; the searing heat turned the iron into a brilliant glow of red that pulsated like a heart. It was pure magic, watching something emerge from fire and a steady hand, a master's hand really. Father was known far and wide throughout Nova Scotia for his skill. Sometimes, as I watched him in his shop, I held my breath for fear breathing itself would cause a wind and such wind would alter the shape he labored over.

He had recently been commissioned to forge rose trellises and a fence gate for the Hardy Family, the wealthiest villagers in River John. Mr. Hardy wanted them finished by Christmas to surprise Mrs. Hardy. Father was grateful for the extra work and hoped to buy a lovely flannel night-gown for Mother that he saw in Hattie's shop window.

"How is your mother doing?" Father would ask as I visited his work shop. But he knew the answer. He saw the weight loss, decline of appetite, sallow skin, how weakened her muscles were becoming. We lifted her from one position to another to make her more comfortable. Each of us continually inquired about her health. As long as we remained concerned we held power over the cancer and could stop it dead in its tracks.

Yes, cancer, I often said to myself, *we are going to get the better of you. This broth for our mother will boot you out of her body; kick you into the deep woods where you will become lost in trees so thick you will never find your way back.* I imagined cancer as the great multiplier, something that insatiably fed itself and thereby replicated itself. If only such industry could be turned to the good, what castles cancer could make.

"Ella, let me show you this, but you must seal your lips, say nothing to Cassie, Abbey or Mother." Father sauntered off to a corner of his shop and returned, holding I knew not what. "It is a candle chandelier to hang over the harvest table," he excitedly announced. "Just think of the fine suppers our family will have underneath the glow of such a magical thing. I know it is a foolish ornament, but once in a while a man is entitled to a bit of foolishness. "

"How lovely," I said. "Mother will cherish it. I can see it hung from a rafter over our table. It will splash lovely flickers of light onto the floor and walls. People never look better than under candlelight. Do you not think so, Father?"

It was then I wondered if my words were true. Would light above us make Mother's face lovely again? Each evening Father carried her to a padded chair at the table and we talked about Father's work and what was going on in River John. We were afraid to ask how she was feeling. The evidence was in. All we had to do was look at her. Even though she attempted cheerfulness, her words were strained.

"I just have a few more trimming ideas." He turned the chandelier carefully in his hands and asked, "How do you think a few pine cones would look on it?"

"That would be most lovely. What about a bird or two?"

"Ella, what a marvelous idea. Yes, a couple of birds would be perfect. I hope to have it finished for the holidays."

He pulled his face protector back on, and slipped into his forging gloves to resume work. His hammer upon the anvil rang its familiar song. The shop smelled of wood smoke and iron. That was exactly what Father smelled like the moment he stepped into the house. It was a good smell, an honest work smell, something that rendered comfort.

"Go check on your mother. Be off with you. I do not want sparks to ruin your clothes or nest in your hair."

I reluctantly opened the door. I really wanted to stay and ask him questions about Doc Williams, what he thought of Mother's weight loss. But the look on his face, a man eager to return to what he knows best, to what he can control, kept me from further questions.

The sun was out giving the endless sea of snow a bluish hue. There was not a single cloud in the sky and the world seemed suddenly expansive.

Oh, blue sky, perfect day, you are a sign things will get better. And I fairly skipped back to the house, holding my dress high to keep from getting a wet ring around the hem. On this lovely day, warmth was primary. The sun shone through my clothes and warmed me as never before.

Once inside, I stoked the fire and put on a kettle for tea. That is when a most marvelous idea struck. I must fetch the lovely beadwork the Micmac gave me; dig it out from between the rocks of the hearth. Something lay in store for the beadwork, of which I had little inkling at the time.

It took a bit of digging with one finger before I held the beadwork in my palm. Yes, I must find the mysterious man whose chants still rang in my ears. The original people were known to have unusual remedies for ailments. They were also known to have some of the best medicine men. Even the village doctors occasionally relied on their cures, but seldom told their patients where they derived such healing properties. No, medical men of esteemed learning would not want the average citizen to think there existed fixes they did not already know about. A doctor liked to think of himself as God-like. For a moment, I, too, wondered what it would be like to prescribe herbal remedies, healing powders.

I pondered how powerful one might feel under such curative circumstances. I so desired to go to a university to study medicine, but alas, as of yet, no girls from our village had ventured upon such a course, no parent willing to believe a daughter worthy of such opportunity. But I am strong headed, and that characteristic could very well land me in a university.

From West Branch to River John

"Father, may I go with you into town on your next delivery trip?"
"Yes, there is a pending delivery, horseshoes I might add, two days hence. You know the Butlers. Their horses are always in need of new hoof-wear," he said as he pulled on his beard and shot me a glance.

"It troubles me," he said. "They challenge those poor beasts summer and winter. I have seen them haul loads no owner should rightfully expect of their animals." He gave a shrug and added, "Mr. Butler will have consequences on Judgment Day due to his treatment of those beasts. There is many an animal he put down due to his own ignorance."

He looked at me again. "Why so urgent, child? You seem excited."

I fidgeted with my hair before saying, "We are out of the blackstrap molasses for holiday cookies. You know how much Cassie and Abbey love to bake molasses cookies."

"It is fine by me, but we must have Abbey stay home from school to attend your mother. Work it out with Abbey."

"Must I? She is ornery as a hornet." Secretly, I felt she would not forgive me for making her remove the buttons off her dress and sew them back on Cassie's dress. Yet, I determined I would ask when she got home from school. I would ply her temperament with promises of cookies. If I wanted to get into town there was no other choice but to do as Father suggested.

It was not the molasses I wanted. What I really wanted was a cure for our mother. Regrettably, such a plan highlighted another lie on *my slate-of-Being,* but it was a lie for the greater good and would, or so was my hope, be weighed differently.

I would need to dress warmly to travel by foot through rough terrain once Father dropped me off. Because of that, two pairs of socks, besides the ones I would wear into River John, seemed prudent. I would roll the extra socks tight and pocket them.

IT IS BEST TO KNOW NOTHING of the future. Upon the first strike of enthusiasm danger might lurk where one least expected it lay in wait.

I set about my plans, fortified myself with the smallest detail. I stuffed nuts and raisins in my pockets to energize my search for Stands Like a Tree. Surely he would know where good medicine was and lead me to it. But I would not have much time, so would quickly dart through snow and over ice in order to return promptly to meet up with Father.

The medicine search day began as all other days. I made porridge for myself and for my sisters, mother and father, as well as tea. The five of us sat at the table, a steady fire blazed its warmth around my bare feet. Mother was so weak she appeared slumped into her shoulders; cheeks with such a white pallor that her features were all but erased. Her voice was a husk of whisper.

"You are looking so much better today," Cassie told her.

Abbey joined in with, "I agree with Cassie. It seems you are much improved. I think the *Soothing Calm* Doc Williams left is taking hold," and she brushed hair from Mother's face, hair that is much like a silver wave upon the sea.

I knew both sisters lied to our mother to cheer her. She was not improved by any medicine. I pondered this deeply. So sometimes an untruth did good? Certainly words held power. Had I not seen that in the works of Robert Burns?

Father finished breakfast first and said, "Be quick, Ella. I have no time to spare for idleness."

Into a handkerchief, I folded up the nuts and raisins and stuffed them into my coat pocket. Cassie was to ride into school later with the neighbors, the MacKay's, their eldest daughter, Hannah, her best friend. Father would make his delivery and I would set out on my search.

Had I any intimation of the difficulty that would soon ensue, I might never have set foot upon such an outlandish effort. There were hints of trouble when Abbey walked to the door with me and squeezed my upper arm with such fierceness I yanked it away. I should have taken that as a warning that dangerous travails were ahead.

"You are a mean little thing," I told her before she slammed the door. "You will pay for your meanness," I yelled back at her through the door.

RIVER JOHN WAS DRAPED in green pine boughs and an occasional red ribbon was tied to storefront posts. The ship builders' sheds were all frosted in fresh snow. Horses stood tethered to posts, their steamy breath making curlicues in the air. A mother and toddler, both bundled in heavy coats and hats, wove their way through snow drifts while several shop owners shoveled their walks, some sprinkling dirt on icy patches. Outside the baker's shop the smell of cinnamon buns wafted in the air like an invitation to happiness.

"Where should I stop?" Father asked.

"Leave me off at Cape John Road near the seamstress's place. Cassie, Abbey and I have a small gift in mind for Mother and I must assist in the making of it. I will meet you back here at what time?" I asked.

"The seamstress's shop is not near the Kitchen Pantry. I thought you were in town to shop for supplies for the Christmas festivities, Ella."

"You're quite right, Father. I just thought a good walk is in order since I have been cooped up in the house for some time. But, I also need to see the seamstress for a special surprise I cannot mention. I am sworn to secrecy."

"All right, young lady. Keep an eye on the church clock. Be back by five in the afternoon." Then he chuckled, "Do not buy too much as you will have to haul it through town from one stop to the next," and he pulled on the reins, but not before inquiring, "Do you have enough money?"

I checked my burlap shopping bag to make sure there was plenty in my purse. "Yes, I have shillings enough. That should be sufficient." After a moment I added, "Do not let Jacob Butler get the better of you when you deliver those trellises and horse shoes. Make sure he puts money straight into your hand and not an I.O.U. note as he usually attempts to get away with. You know how difficult it is to get paid up by some folks who actually have more than we do." This annoyed my mother and I was simply voicing what she herself would say if she were here with us.

He winked at me, a sparkle in his eyes, and took his time prompting the horses towards the Butler's place up on Pictou Road, the drays' curls of breath steaming in the air.

ELLA SETS FORTH

Each year, from December to April the basin of River John freezes over. Massive sheets of ice back into each other so tightly they look like skinned and stacked fish from afar. But I have no need to cross that treacherous terrain nor have I ever done so; no, I will instead head in the opposite direction to Minnie's farmhouse and enquire where Stands Like a Tree might be.

Minnie, unfortunately, has been scorned by the more pious villagers. They consider her crazy. Light in the head is how they put it. But unbeknownst to them she is a wise woman who listens closely to the heartbeat of the land. Often, I have visited with her at church suppers and lingered, listening to her stories about gardening and putting up preserves. Her husband died of smallpox the year the disease struck the coastal village and she decided to stay on by herself at the home they had built, forging a life of independence.

The church folks have been worried that she would be taken by illness or by the Indians, living by her own means on the outskirts of town. Instead, she has befriended many of the original families, made warm clothing for their children, and shared what she grows in her garden and has laid aside in her root cellar. Because of her goodness the First Nation peoples watch out for her.

If I am fortunate enough to receive the blessings of my Maker, I want to live into old age, become like Minnie with wisps of gray hair clustered at my neck, and I especially hope to express a friendly countenance. My hands will busy themselves on behalf of others; ten fingers for seven days of the week can add up to something.

Chimney smoke billows from Minnie's home, the white pick-et-fence nearly buried in snow. I reach into my pocket to make certain the extra socks have not bounced free. Noises come from inside the house so I knock extra hard. The door swings open and there stands a woman so short you might mistake her for a child, her apron snug over her homespun shift.

Her face is apple red, a color sometimes noticed in others, especially women of a certain age. She wears a mobcap like so many women wear to keep their hair from getting dirty.

"Sit," Minnie says, and indicates with her hand which chair to take. She quickly goes back to chopping kindling for her stove.

"What brings you out here to the farm?"

"My mother is sick. She is wasting away. There is nowhere else to go. Do you know how to reach Stands Like a Tree?" But before she answers I further explain myself.

"I thought maybe he traveled upland like his people do when winter arrives, but I have never seen their villages, their birch bark wigwams. Each fall they pack up their birch canoes and head for the hills, their belongings stored in canoes. My sisters and I sometimes see them pass on Father's property. So I know they must be in the nearby hills."

"Yes, yes, I have seen all that. What do you want from Stands Like a Tree?"

"I have to ask him if he knows of a cure for my mother. Doc Williams' cure is doing her no good. She has become thin as a stick doll."

Minnie put down the hatchet and pulled a chair in front of me. She took both my hands in her rough hands and looked so pensively into my eyes I thought she could see inside my skull where my brain is cradled. Perhaps she was even reading my thoughts.

On the windowsills sat wizened roots, beets and turnips. I marveled at the mustiness of her place and concluded the decaying roots and herbs she kept stirred up an odor that permeated her house, yet it was a scent full of delightful mystery. I would feel terrible if she knew people in town said that her house was made of musk, something so pungent that it was offensive. They snickered behind her back. "Yes, I heard from Elder Sutherland who conducts the Sabbath in the Bigney District that your mother has taken ill." She turned my hands over, and looked at them. "Fine china hands," she said and added, "I am sorry to hear of your mother's plight. God works in mysterious ways."

I dismissed her statement about God. As far as I was concerned his mysterious ways were filled with pain and suffering.

"What am I to do?" I asked her, and pulled my hands back into my lap. "I have great trepidation over God's ways."

"Mind your tongue, girl. Does your father know you are out here on your own?"

"No, he thinks I am shopping for the holidays."

"What makes you think I know Stands Like a Tree's whereabouts? And what makes you think I will not march you straight back into town so your father can give you a good scolding?"

"Minnie, you are my only hope. I met Stands Like a Tree on the ice in early December. Billy, you know Billy O'Flannigan, taunted him and I intervened. Stands Like a Tree told me I was made of the stars as he turned me back towards my friends. There was a power in his hands I will not soon forget. He placed each hand on my shoulders as he turned me to face the others. An unexplainable energy passed through his palms, a healing energy."

"That is all you are going by, young lady?" She smoothed her hands down over her apron. "That does not seem wise," she added.

"No, he also gave me a lovely brooch made with quills and beads. When he placed it in my hand he said, `Should you ever need me seek me out.'"

"I do not like the feel of this," Minnie said, her eyes downcast, shoulders sinking into her body. "You do not know the lay of the land in these parts. How long do you think this excursion will take?"

"Well, it is mid-morning now and I expect to be back in River John, providing all goes well, to fetch supplies around three. At the very least I can make inquiry into Stands Like a Tree's whereabouts and perhaps find him at a future date. I know the Micmac people are not far from here. Stands Like a Tree told Hadley the baker that they were camped about a mile from your place."

She fidgeted a moment, "You are quite right, that is where they are. But you must first promise to return by three. I have a bad feeling about this, but I also recognize the importance of your pursuit. The Micmac People are a mile out from Old Station Road and to the left of Split Lightning Tree. I cannot guarantee Stands Like a Tree will be there. There has been talk of his negotiating with the Mohawks."

"Thank you, Minnie. I am grateful for your help." I wanted to hug her but reserve held me back. Minnie was not a woman you threw extravagance upon. No, she was the frugal sort who would scorn an outburst of emotion.

Minnie walked me to the door, looked at the sky and said, "You had best hurry. Those clouds off Sunrise Trail make their own predictions. Hasten, my girl."

The door closed behind me with a slight wheeze. I waved to Minnie who stood in the kitchen window, hands clasped to her face. Here I was about to embark on a journey that would cause much consternation and that would test my fortitude. But it is a good thing we cannot see into our future. Many would turn back at their first peek.

THE DANGER TIME

Little did I know what peril I was about to heap upon myself—the chilling cold that would cut through my clothes; the sting from bushes that would slap back with a vicious snap. Nor did I foresee the worry that would cloud my house.

The unruly temperament of the wind started to pick up. Oh, a thousand castigations upon my soul for surely I am ready to embark on the impossible.

I was also about to enter upon another lie.

Little powdery puffs of snow dance across the horizon, delicate and light as they land upon the nose.

I hasten to make good time. *Don't dawdle*, rings in my ears. But I am amazed when attempting to hurry my feet turn stubbornly slow. My expectations are not able to catch up with my will.

"Clodhopper," I tell myself. "You are but a clodhopper."

In the distance, clouds cluster in angry gray masses. The sky speaks to me in pictures that are sometimes quite remarkable. That is one of the joys of being near the Northumberland Straits. Miles of water offer the sky a drink and the sky is sometimes very thirsty, especially come summer. It is the sky's thirst that creates the clouds and I wonder what my thirst for a cure means. Does it mean I will become a doctor?

"Stay focused, look for Split Lightning Tree," I remind myself. The air is crisp against my cheeks. When I find Stands Like a Tree will I become tongue tied? This puzzles me and for a moment certitude that I am a foolish young woman in search of a cure takes its strangling hold. I reach for my raisins; let each one grow plump underneath my tongue before swallowing.

Crows huddle on a fence and scold each other with raspy voices. Their black feathers shine against the gray canopy above them. There seems no more common a bird in all the land than the back yard crow. But they are survivors—a most hardy bird. Their caw-caws can become annoying. There is no bird this side of Halifax that chatters to such extravagant excess.

Mr. and Mrs. Larson wave as they drive by in their horse-drawn wagon packed with supply-barrels that jostle from slippery spots in the road. The barrels are not tethered properly and it is a wonder they do not spill their entire goods. Mrs. Larson wears a long over-coat and has a caramel colored scarf around her shoulders as well as a blanket over her lap. Mr. Larson tips his hat to me and hollers, "Take care, Ella. Better hasten home promptly. Those clouds warn of a storm headed our way. There will be snow aplenty this year."

We already have a couple of feet—the gods never fail to drop moisture upon our land so it comes as no surprise there will be more.

A chilling fear runs down my spine. I hope the Larsons do not run into Father, tell him of my whereabouts. I have only a short way to go, but unfortunately it is all uphill before I reach the road that leads to the tree Minnie mentioned. The road is called Cemetery Drive, but I doubt the dead buried there take their carriages or sleighs out. Ghosts are not capable of steering anything. Their limbs are bound— inertia at the heart of their souls. Inside myself, I practice what to say to Stands Like a Tree.

Do you know of the whereabouts of a medicine man? Do you have herbs that might heal my ailing mother? I have nothing to give you in return other than a promise that should you ever need assistance, I will promptly return the favor. If you have to travel far in search of healing properties, would you kindly deliver them directly to my home? If so, it is best to make any delivery mid-afternoon and down by the stables. I live in West Branch River John next to the MacKay family. Please stay clear of their place as their grandfather was shot by one of your people years back. They fail to see what my heart now concludes. There is good in all kinds of people.

The Micmacs are never far from our home. Father often councils my sisters and myself to be respectful of all people. He says each man must be judged upon his own merits. Many a Micmac has helped the settlers and they are not the trouble suggested by some of the villagers. I do keep in mind though that some few settlers have been raided, and far worse, a few have been killed. What would I do if strangers from across the sea came insisting my land was theirs?

SNOW THAT BLINDS

Swirls of snow pick up speed, nearly blinding me in their urgent sweep across my face. I dream of a cup of tea laced with clover honey. The air smells like wet wool or perhaps I have caught scent of myself. I tire trudging uphill. Shadows behind trees stoke my imagination; a tight grip clasps my chest. Perhaps a gunshot from French trappers will suddenly strike me down. Foolish thought. Solace yourself with the knowledge that a peaceful girl in search of a cure is no threat and therefore is protected by whatever angels exist.

The twelve o'clock bell rings faintly from the church which is now far behind. Its familiarity renders small comfort. Split Lightning Tree lies ahead and its halved, fallen trunk seems a pathetic animal unable to crawl to safety. I let out a sigh, pleased to be almost there. Looking ahead to the left, there is a path that cuts through the forest. That must be the place Minnie mentioned. For but a few minutes I sit on the split tree bough and nibble an oat-cake. After a short respite, I wrap the remaining cake and tuck it back into my pocket.

Fear crouches like a wild animal in my chest. *Gather your wits, girl,* I tell myself. Not only is the path dark with trees crowded on both sides, but worry also lurks inside me, clawing at my innards. Who would have known that fear could make my boots so heavy and ponderous? *Oh, foolish girl, you are on a self-inflicted errand that could lead to trouble.*

With that in mind, I enter the tree world, clutching my coat as though it might steady me. Bushes snap across my face and take me aback. I wipe where one hit, my mitten tainted with a string of blood.

Wind shakes the tree branches into a clicking chatter. Snow pelts downward at a slant. Stark boughs scratch across the sky.

I cross Stone Hill Creek, known for its shallow water, frozen mounds of snow crunching under foot, and head up an incline bordered with hemlock and pines. A rabbit scampers into the woods. Deer tracks slowly fill in with snow and my own tracks begin to disappear when I look back. To pacify myself, I recall a story told by my grandfather of the early settlers.

TWO YOUNG GENTLEMEN set off for Halifax to purchase potatoes, so terribly weak from lack of food, they could scarcely walk and were nearly ready to give up. In the woods they discovered trout spread out to dry on a bush, the fisherman they presumed not far. They hesitated from fear of their intended thievery, but hunger prevailed and they snatched the fish and ran, eating them raw on the run. When they got to Halifax the only potatoes available to them were filled with worms, fit only for cattle. So hungry were their families upon their return that they dug up potato splits to eat.

No, I am fortunate that today we are much more comfortable than our ancestors who arrived on the Hector, all of them promised cattle and sheep and splendid farms. But when they emigrated from Scotland to Nova Scotia they were met with unbroken forests so thick that a man had to chop his way through. There was only a tipsy building into which all newcomers were housed. There were no cows, as promised, nothing in their contract was delivered and some of the settlers became so distraught they sat down and cried at their lot.

When supplies did finally come through, the emigration agents refused to give the settlers what was promised and kept all the goods for themselves. Eighteen on board the Hector died. Most were children and women. They were buried at sea before landing in this great country. Several of those who did make it here later died of disappointment or illness.

⇆

THE TREES SLOW THE WIND. Here, I am sheltered by their closeness. How far I have walked eludes me, and I am now far from any church bells. Hopefully, I am closer to my destination but I have no way of knowing with any certainty. The fresh air makes me sleepy and I long to nest underneath a tree for but a short while.

London Bridge is Falling Down

Step off the beaten path for a moment and you are lost. Step off the beaten path and you are doomed. There are places where one should not tread and there are penalties extracted for doing so.

I would like to talk with Robert Burns right about now. Would he think me a foolish girl? One cannot count on poetry deep in the woods, or maybe poetry comes from the deep woods. Beautiful mushrooms unfold their parasols each summer and they too prompt a lyric or two. I have so many questions for Robbie Burns. First, does he think I have the makings of a poet? I will repeat for him the start of one I wrote:

Down in the grove where the graves run deep
Down where the footfalls of spirits
Aimlessly walk in their sleep
Down where mothers lie atop graves and weep

I cannot remember more of my verse, but it is safe at home in my ledger and hopefully my sisters do not discover it. They are nosey little things. I once caught Cassie thumbing through my ledger. Her excuse, "Why, Ella, you left it out for so long, I thought you wanted me to read the page it was opened to. After all, you often ask my opinion when you read a new poem aloud."

If all the words in the world fell like snow what would they taste like and what would they smell like? Could I make a necklace of them and adorn all creatures of earth with alphabet jewelry. For the swan I would apply v's to its feathers. The cows would wear o's that sparkle in the sunshine, and sheep would wear the very letter their species starts with. I would line up all the various animals and make complete words of them, and then move on to sentences that would convey the amazing beauty the earth bestows.

But, here I daydream and must not. Yet an idle mind withers into a dried-out walnut, but hopefully there is little chance of that with mine. To me, daydreaming is exercise for the brain. One of my grandmothers forgot to employ her brain to the full service of her body and because of that she became an empty hull.

She sat silent for hours in the rocker, an absent expression on her face, her eyes much like the very first gray polliwogs of summer. Mind you, I never said anything to Father about this observation. He would not have tolerated such comparisons. Hopefully, it is not unkind to measure a person's characteristics. How else does one determine who one wants to become? It takes a process of elimination and addition to make a soul. To console myself lest I find myself too critical, I often soothed her brow and made her tea. I held my impressions to myself, not even sharing my opinion with friends.

All this is much idle thought. If I could sit and rest for a moment my journey would run smoother. But Father always warns that if we are in the woods in winter to resist the urge to rest, to keep walking no matter how tired we become. He says many people have succumbed to the cold and never awakened. Still, a small reprieve seems most delectable.

I veer from the path to sit for but a minute and eat my raisins. A felled log with a little roof of branches lies just ahead. Snow still falls, although it has tapered off. I slog through the snow and just as I am about to sit on the log a sharp snapping sound alarms me. I jerk my head back, fearful that the noise might have come from someone in the woods, but there is no one visible through the wall of trees.

Where did such noise come from? Pain in my ankle rises and makes me think I may have stepped into buried berry bushes with their nail-like thorns or pushed my foot through a sharp rim of ice.

But on closer look, *Oh no, I have stepped into a leg trap. What, oh what, am I to do?*

Quickly, I slip off my mittens and pry at the jaws of the contraption. My fingers are icy cold and the jaws unyielding. With both hands I attempt to spring myself free. The trap's steel teeth are cold and tear at my fingers, droplets of blood smear the snow, but it will not loosen even a bit. To lose a limb to free myself would never be an option. Animals are known to chew off limbs in order to liberate themselves, but that idea is out for me. *Dern the trappers. Dern the fur traders.* I am caught like an animal, no yank or pull strong enough to spring me free.

Now I know why Father says that leghold traps should be outlawed. He once found a young raccoon in trouble, its leg nearly chewed off. He carried it home in his jacket pocket and we kept it in a crock pot and made a splint for its leg. When the coon healed we moved it to the barn where the cats mothered it. Father forbade us to name it since it would be returned to the wild, but I secretly called the raccoon Scotty, and whispered its name into its soft ear. But that was back in safety-time and here I am with an unimaginable dilemma looming in front of me.

I bite my lips. The ankle pain is severe. It courses through my body making me even colder. The day seems a raw, savage beast. If I dig out the chain that holds the trap, I might free myself and hobble for help. The chain eludes my grasp. My fingers grow numb with cold as they poke underneath the log, searching for the chain.

What is this? It is the screw head that tethers the legtrap. With all my might I attempt to work it free but it will not budge. My hands are so cold they have turned blue. I brace my free foot against a nearby tree and pull harder at the screw. It still does not budge. *Scream, scream,* I tell myself. Perhaps someone will hear you, but that possibility is small. Only the trees witness my plight and they are no help whatsoever. *You must rest, I tell myself.* But rest does not easily come when fear and pain co-mingle like old friends. Tears swell and blind me.

Oh, what will I do? I wipe my tears onto the cuff of my coat. The thought of sleeping here over night chills me to the bone. My parents come to mind, my mother sick, all of them worried about me. Oh, for sure, they will find out I strayed from town and never again trust me.

If I am still here by nightfall I will be frozen stiff come morning. *You must move your limbs, even the toes, or they will harden to wood.* I stand to stretch, careful not to further injure my trapped foot and flap my arms like a bird. Yet, it is difficult to stand, to move even the short distance within which I can move. *Steady now,* I tell myself. *Steady. Fear reaps nothing. Didn't Father often say that?*

How much time has passed, I cannot fathom. The edge of day begins to darken, nighttime's arrival always earlier in the woods. What sky can be seen through the trees is ash gray and even though the snow has all but let up there are boulders of clouds that promise further storms. To keep my spirits up, I begin to sing a song my sisters and I often sing:

London Bridge is broken down,
Falling down, falling down.
London Bridge is falling down,
My fair lady
Build it up with wood and clay,
Wood and clay, wood and clay,
Build it up with wood and clay,

My fair lady, I remind myself to get up and at least sway, clapping my hands to keep time with the words I sing to stay warm—my weight held by the free leg. My mittens smother sound as one hand hits against the other making little puffs of noise. *Oh, be of cheerful heart. Do not dally in the halls of fright. Sing, sing to your heart's content. Sing loud enough so that someone will hear you.*

Wood and clay will wash away,
Wash away, wash away,
Wood and clay will wash away,
My fair lady

Build it up with bricks and mortar,
Bricks and mortar, bricks and mortar,
Build it up with bricks and mortar,
My fair lady.

Certainly I am no fair lady since I have once again told an untruth. No matter how hard I try, my spirits remain dampened. Again, I cry, my ankle snared in the throat of the beast and throbbing more severely. I yank the chain that holds the trap in place but to no good. There is nothing to be done except yell. At the top of my lungs I shout for help. My whole body backs me up and sends my voice far. It flies like a bird. The more my frustration grows and my words melt away like idle snowflakes the quieter the woods become.

Yes, Father will be looking for me in River John. What if you never make it out of these woods? What if you are eaten by wolves? Those thoughts make me scream louder for help until my throat is sore, the way it feels after I eat rhubarb. But there is no voice loud enough to penetrate what darkness fortifies these thick woods.

Slowly, I brush snow from the log and sit back down, mindful of my entrapped foot. To keep the circulation going, I rub the upper part of my leg and comfort myself with the remaining raisins. Shots of pain shoot through me, and thoughts of the man from Toney River who lost his leg to gangrene haunt me. No doctor will saw my leg off, but it is far more likely I will freeze to death before that option. I remind myself to keep my circulation in motion by moving around. Dumb animal, tethered to disaster's post.

A poem Mother often recites by Goldsmith comes to mind and it perfectly reflects how lonely these woods have become and what they now represent:

When looking round, the lonely settler sees
His home amid a wilderness of trees;
How sinks his heart in those deep solitudes,
Where not a voice upon his ear intrudes

Did my mother feel this lonely? How little she has revealed of what she thinks. It is as though the need to survive surpasses everything. Little expression of doubt or conflict ever falls upon her lovely face. There must be much thought and many feelings she keeps from her daughters, and yet the sickness is something she cannot hide. I wish she were nearby, holding me in her arms. I am frightfully afraid as night encroaches. Even the stark branches seem to scratch the sky as though trees, too, were caught in a frozen trap. With all my heart I pray and feel ashamed of my previous questioning the Lord. Yet, nagging doubt persists. There is no way on earth to understand the suffering of others. If there were a benevolent God, why would such a being let creatures endure so many tribulations? It makes no sense.

Freezing to death must be like falling into water. I am less afraid of freezing. But the water, well that is quite another story.

WATER'S ENDLESS TUNNEL

Water rubs against me as though it were my best friend. It swirls and little bubbles burst about as though the happiest chaps in the world. The shadow of Father's fishing boat drifts aimlessly above me—a clotted crow on water. Father, himself, is dangling over the boat's side and then sinking further, I can no longer see him. My chest feels it will implode. I cannot breathe without taking in large gulps of water. I hold my breath. Clothes bind me in a death sheet. With one foot I push free my shoe and then cast off the other.

We have been fishing for cod, but something bigger bit and Father asked me to untangle the line from the oar hold. That was folly of the worst kind. A wave struck just as I stood and over I went, a terrible topsy-turvy sight, my father hollering Ella, Ella, and then there was only the dark and the deep where sound was the sound of my swishing hands fitfully churning to lift to the water's surface. *Keep to your senses, girl. You know how to swim.* But it felt as though I were being swallowed by the darkness in the Northumberland Straits.

My clothes bound me and I ripped at them trying to free myself until only my petticoat remained. And I knew about drowning, its fateful toll on our village. Shipping vessels and dories were struck by vicious storms and sank from sight. In honor of the lost fishermen, local fog-horns played their bellowing sound that floated across water as though an ill omen for all villagers—*take heed, take heed, this, too, could come to you.*

Well, that was not for me. Not drowning. What of all my careful eating, refusal of second helpings—my attempts to escape the watchful eye of death? No, I will outrun death even here in the water. But I grew so fretful over sharks and whales and things that cannot be seen. I thought of eels rubbing against me and a chill rose, a chill so horrid it nearly stopped me from inching upward.

Afterwards, there were nightmares of endless dunkings. Sometimes the much talked about Killer Whales who feed in the Straights through the summer stalked me. Sometimes, in my dreams, American Eels bound me with their pliant and powerful bodies, dragging me down into the creature filled depths. I would wake, screaming and gasping for air. But, no matter how forceful the spill into the Northumberland Straights, I always, always surfaced.

Stubborn, I am willfully stubborn and that perhaps is what saved me. Father simply reached down and hefted me into the boat's safety, kissing my brow over and over. There I was, a girl of fourteen, cradled in her father's arms. He rocked me back and forth as though I were a small child. "Oh, Ella, you caused me much concern. I thought you were gone." We headed straight for home—no more fishing that day, nor any other day for me.

CARRIED BY THE WIND

Someone swings. It is not me. Someone swings and she is light as air. The wind kisses her cheeks, rubs its nose with her nose. She feels someone's heart nearby. It drums against her face, smooths the creases of her forehead. Someone is wearing sage. She recognizes the herb because it reminds her of holidays. Oh, who could it be? This young woman carried by the wind and soft as a chick? There is a scent of balsam in the air. She is warm as she swings. In this sleepy world there is no fear.

If she wanted, she could leap across great distances like an elk sprung free by a hunter. Summer shines down upon her. Here there are no storms, no wolves in search of prey, no hardship of any kind. Here, she is daughter of the angels and she wears a gown like theirs. It is flowing white, a braided gold tassel belt is tied at her waist and her shoes are made of silk. Her hair, too, is silk and hangs to the ground. Her loosened hair dusts the earth, a small rustling sound as it sweeps over ferns.

All the things she has heard of death are true. It is blue. Soft baby blue.

Here, sight is not seeing. Sight is feeling. It is as if every pore of her body became song, a harp somewhere in the distance plays the most beautiful melody. Here, the edge of the world is lit with flowers and no foghorn blows to announce another ship down. The world smells like honey and evergreen of the finest quality. There is a golden light that beckons at the end of a tunnel. It is the most beautiful thing she has ever seen. She is floating toward that light, that most splendid star of heaven. And she is weightless. A breath of warm air spills over her, bathes her.

At the very edge of sight golden flecks sprinkle downward. She is covered in gold speckles, it tickles her nose, and the closer she nears the end of the tunnel the more radiant things become and the more splendid the music; the most plaintive melody she has ever heard, pools of tears form in her eyes.

There is an urge to move forward, yet something mysterious tugs her back. She is like a bird on a bough tethered to the infinite. And the light, the incredible light shining through splashes into a rainbow. Everything inside her wants to float towards that radiance but something holds her back.

She wants traction in the infinite, a place to wedge her foot in the splendid world of unseen possibility.

Breaking into Light

"Here child, sip this barley water." An undefined figure flutters above me, the face entirely out of focus. Someone is gently cradling my neck, fingers firm as they hold something warm to my mouth. There are voices that rise and grow silent; a continual breathing of words and murmurs. It feels like the room is on fire. Or, am I on fire?

Someone says, "Wash her ankle with vinegar. Pound sumac roots to soften them and tuck them in as a poultice around her ankle. Keep her still for a few days. If she shows signs of a persistent fever have someone fetch me. But do not let her amble about. She is a bull-headed one."

My blankets rise and lower with each breath. Hands frequently tuck covers in around me as I toss and turn. It is as though my body were somehow cast to a raging sea. Hair that smells of sage falls into my face, brushes lightly across my cheek making me sneeze. Or perhaps I have been sneezing for a long time and have just become aware of it. But the hair smells familiar—steeped with scent of the woods. Yes, hair floated into my face in a dream—hair that smelled of hemlock and blue spruce. Or was it sage?

"She will do well if you keep her warm and give her plenty of fluids." The voice sounds just like my mother's doctor. Then another voice breaks in, one that carries the rivers and wind in each word. No, it cannot be Stands Like a Tree. The voice says, "She is a strong girl made from the stars."

Another voice asks, "Have her parents been notified?"

A long silence follows the question. Words again take to the air like so many birds. The voice sounds like Doc Williams, "If I can get through with my team of horses, I plan on going out to Ebenezer's tomorrow, providing the storm abates. I will notify them their daughter has been found and is presumed to make a full recovery, providing, of course, she remains warm and off her feet until that ankle heals."

If I have been found then where have I been? Worry snaps like a cornered, wild animal. It shunts fear through my chest. Where am I? My eyes struggle to open wide but a smidgen of sight makes me dizzy. I cannot push myself up onto my elbows to look around. "Lie still," a voice intercepts any struggle. The world somehow is set to a slant. I remember an earlier darkness of wind and then a floating sensation. Oh, where have I gone? Have I done something wrong?

This world of little definition is most enchanting. It is warm here. Robert Burns visits me and recites his work. His voice is melodic. We talk about poetry and what he thinks it takes to become a fine poet. His eyes are so alive, so animated, that they too speak. His hair is wildly thrown over his brow and his nose is red from imbibing in spirits. His whole body moves as he speaks, keeping time to the cadence of his words.

He tells me he loves Scotland above all other places in the world—the glens, the dales. And he loves to be in love. I imagine many women are smitten by him. Those eyes. Those eyes. A man's eyes could be a curse as well as a blessing.

Any dreaming of mine is violently broken into. "Give her some wormwood steeped in water later in the day. When she is fully awake have her drink large quantities of orange mint tea. The more tea the better. As I said, if I can get to West Branch, I will drop in on her folks. Weather permitting, of course. I want to check on her mother too."

"An outright blizzard out there right now." A door opens and closes; a rush of cold air sweeps into the room and the door bangs shut. Someone's hand sweeps across my forehead. It is a musty hand.

My stomach growls. I dream of stewed meats, Indian bread, cakes and pudding. I also dream of a blackstrap molasses cookie with a cup of freshly drawn warm milk to dunk the sweet in—but only one cookie for me because I must go as one invisible. Was I not about to buy some things in town for the upcoming holidays?

Is my head frozen? Perhaps I am in heaven and cannot recognize the place from lack of experience. How could I possibly recognize it? I have never been there. And who says I would even get to that place reserved for the most pious and goodly souls? Perhaps the devil has something in store for me—a pitchfork to prod me with, hail and brimstone to shower me with. After all, it slowly occurs to me, someone disobeyed her parents by going out on the ice the night of the skate dance. Have I, again, wronged? Was I on my way somewhere?

I want to get up but cannot. Oh my flesh and bones, are you inert as a dead mouse? Someone is babbling. Her words make no sense. Who mumbles, "The lambs of the flock are fed with the milk of the word?" Were those words were spoken at sermon last Sunday?

Pastor Smith is most meticulous in his speech. I imagine him writing and then scribbling out most of what he writes. He is a man who is never satisfied with his writing or with his parishioners. He claims we are nearly bound for hell if we do not mend our ways. He has a kindly side though, one that shines through on rare occasions. I must keep the kindly side of his nature in mind.

What a blathering idiot. I have missed Sunday School. More important, I might have missed school, too. Oh, the headmaster, Hector Adams, will be very irritated with me. He asked me, Ella, to load the school's stove with coal this week and strike up a fire to warm the room so that we can comfortably begin our lessons.

Father said he could watch Mother for a week because work is slack just before the holidays. Each week someone from our class is assigned to starting the stove. Mr. Adams strikes us on the knuckles with a yardstick for forgetfulness or tardiness. I must get up, not lie abed all day, and start the headmaster's fire.

It occurs to me that Schoolmaster Adams is not a kind man. His eyes glint with pleasure when he strikes one of us. When the boys misbehave, he takes them to the coal shed and gives them a good strapping. I told Father this and he said I must mind my ways at all times. He also says to inform him if the schoolmaster takes any of the female students to the woodshed.

Our schoolmaster reads a book aloud as though he enjoyed tormenting the pages. I cannot understand why the sheets of text have not torn free from every book he reads. When he calls on me to recite French, he says:*Ella MacKinnon, stand and recite from memory today's lesson. Louder, so the whole class can hear.* He usually pauses before saying: *How many times do I have to stress your posture? Stand straight girl. A crooked spine will harm your growth and interfere with your breathing.* Then he wipes his snooty nose on a much maligned handkerchief. I do not think he has heard of soap and water. On second thought, he needs a good bar of lye to get the dirt off him.

Wiry hair, stiff as spears, shoot from his ears. He must have a garden of weeds in them. We secretly call him Wire Ears. His ears are his weak spot. They once swelled so badly from infection that he put roasted onions in them as a cure and took to his bed early. He confided this before French class and all of us snickered. Schoolmaster Adams was so absorbed in articulating his lessons that he took no notice of our bad manners. Sometimes, though rarely, I feel sorry for him and give him a treat from my lunch.

French is my favorite study. I imagine myself in Paris, an exotic place I have learned much about from *The Tinder*, our weekly newspaper. I would make friendships with all the artists in France. Father says they live a reckless life, drink a substance called absinthe. I am not interested in what they drink, but I would like to catch their sparks of creativity and ignite myself.

Also, the French dress is much more flamboyant—they seldom wear formless linen shifts, with square collars, like we do here in Nova Scotia. The French women dress to be noticed. But that part I can do without in order to press on as one unnoticed. That way, God cannot catch up with me. I do not want to be put in the earth like a lowly ground mole.

⊷

As THE HOURS IDLY PASS, someone floats like a cloud in and out of life. That someone is me. What a dreamy world I settle into. There is little break in my dreams, save the tea occasionally pressed to my lips. I swallow large gulps as though a fire stoked my thirst. The tea must have honey in it because it is sweet.

I recognize the voice that coaxes me to drink. Did I not hear it a while back? Even though this dreamy feeling is much like a soft quilt, I now feel somewhat tired of it. It offers little challenge and I am someone who likes challenges.

Minnie Miller Intervenes

"Here Ella, let me help you to sit up." She props plump pillows behind my back. It appears, to my surprise, I am in Minnie's house. For the life of me I cannot figure why. All of her jars of preserves sit in the windows and catch what little winter light comes from outside. There are a few turnips too, potatoes with ugly white sprouts, elephant trunks my sisters and I call them, as well as shriveled beets on the window sills. There is also the familiar musty smell—herbs and old things dug up from the earth.

Now, I remember setting out in search of a cure and how Minnie gave me directions to the Micmac village. The air in her house is purple or perhaps the light makes it appear so. I am in a makeshift bed directly across from the fire in the hearth. My bed is made out of a shipping box from one of the builders in River John. Little hay whiskers stick out from the burlap mattress which Minnie made with hay and cast off bags stored in the nearby barn. I nearly laugh when I look over the side of the bed and see the words, "Fresh, Ice Packed Salmon."

"So, I am salmon now," I tell her.

"Watch out for splinters," Minnie warns. She leaves me for a moment and comes back with a piece of broad flannel cloth that she promptly tucks around the upper wooden frame of the box. "That will save you from splinters. We do not need further irritants on top of what has already befallen you in the woods."

"Why am I here, Minnie?"

"Do you not remember getting your foot caught in a trap, child? You nearly caught your death out there. Perhaps your mind is playing tricks on you."

"Oh, Minnie, I did not get what I set out for; herbs for my mother." Everything begins to clear in my memory. "My poor parents must be worried to death. I have heaped much concern upon them. How long have I been here?"

"Around two days. We cannot safely notify your parents of your whereabouts until the storm clears."

"Two days! That cannot be."

"You nearly froze to death out there. A few more hours and you would have died. Lucky for you, Stands Like a Tree was returning home from his meeting with the Mohawks."

Minnie is seated near the fire, a contented look on her face. When she becomes content all her wrinkles disappear and radiance lights her face. The wooden hooks click while she crochets a pillowcase fringe that trails off onto the floor. She saves the string from flour and sugar sacks for transformation into, what she calls, the unnecessary "little beauties" for her house.

Such frugality is required in these parts. My mother, too, saves string, admonishes my sisters and me should we throw out a single piece. She makes lace for our petticoats and pillows. She dyes the string with beets and herbs, her hands the color of the dyes for days afterwards, the most vivid hues imbedded in the lines of her palms. Sometimes I turn her hands over in mine and with a finger I follow those lines. I tell her they are a route to her heart, that under-hands are the heart's map. She tells me to stop such frivolous talk, that I am mystery to her.

"My parents need to know I am here."

"That is being taken care of. Doc Williams will head his team of horses out to West Branch as soon as weather permits. He has promised to notify them of your whereabouts."

"I am going to get up and go tell them myself." My leg, the one that was caught in the trap, is so heavy it cannot move. I twist it from side to side and try to swing it over the side of the bed, all to no avail. It has become just like the log I sat on when attempting to undo the trap.

"You will do no such thing. Doc Williams plans to get word to them himself. It is your strong-headedness that gets you into trouble;

besides, I kind of like the idea of a borrowed daughter, especially since I have no surviving children of my own."

"How come? It is easy enough, so Mother says." Minnie's face clouded as she reached back into her life.

"God did not see fit to make one that could endure these winters." She put down her crochet hooks as though they suddenly became too heavy, her face clouded.

"My first baby, Thomas, died in his cradle at two months and the other died at birth. It nearly broke my heart. Mr. Miller, my husband, said, ' "That is it. I cannot take such loss again. We will do fine just the two of us.'" He was a good man, Ella. He always provided the necessaries even when times were tough. Mr. Miller said it was no use to pile on more agony." She looked at the door as though Mr. Miller might suddenly saunter in. Minnie gathered her dress, hoisted it up to keep it from sweeping over the slate floor. She hustled over to the cast iron pot that hung above the hearth. When she removed the lid a most wonderful venison smell filled the air. She carefully stirred and ladled the broth over the meat and sprinkled some thickening flour into it.

"Stands Like a Tree brought me this venison after he carried you to my house. He has a thoughtful nature. In the summertime he picks berries and drops off a basket-full. Sometimes I make him a berry pie. He always insists we eat a piece together before he takes the pie back to his place."

Now I vividly recall Stands Like a Tree on the ice that fateful night. There was power in his body and his raven hair shone like brook water when moonlight hits it. So he was the one who freed me from the leg trap? He was the one who carried me to safety. What can I do for him in return? I will have to ask Father if he has extra tins of maple syrup.

"I am figuring a healthy helping of this stew will give you strength," Minnie says. "You look like you lost ten pounds out there in your snowy oasis."

Suddenly, hunger stirred in my belly. I also grew worried. My family, how upset they must be. Was my mother doing better? Had color returned to her face? I also feared the terrible admonishments ahead. One forfeits something for telling an untruth. What will they take away? And does it really matter? If I can keep my mother alive nothing else on this earth is as important. Perhaps they will understand that my absence was motivated by search for a cure.

MINNIE LADLES OUT THE STEW, sprinkles some salt on it, and pulls a chair to my bedside. Upon the chair's seat she places my stew bowl, a crochet trimmed homespun napkin, a jar of milk and some soda biscuits. Next, she pulls a chair up for herself, fetches a bowl and sits near me. Wisps of gray hair, so grey they are like hoar-frost, settle along her neckline. Peach fuzz softens her cheeks. Never have I seen such a lovely face. Trouble and sorrow have visited Minnie, but grief has not set her face to stone. That is how I will live. No matter what comes my way, I must surpass all the trials and tribulations set forth. No, I will not dally in the halls of remorse.

Time is a worthless crumb if one wallows in self pity. I will have none of that. "Buck up, girl, I tell myself. Buck up for what awaits you."

"Tell me Minnie, how long will my leg feel heavy as an anvil?"

"That is a question you will have to take up with Doc Williams when he comes by after seeing your parents. I suppose your father will soon follow him."

"You should take a few steps today." Minnie continues, "That is what the doctor said. I aim to loan you my shoulder for support. You are most fortunate you did not break your ankle. Once you finish eating, we will start working that leg and afterwards I will wrap fresh poultice around it."

Minnie clears the dishes and helps me to the side of the bed. She offers me her arm. Surprise hits me that I am so unsure on my feet. The first few steps send ripples of pain through my leg and up into my hip. We walk several times to the butter churn by the pantry and back. Minnie grunts a little as though, she too, hauled a wounded leg.

Once back in the safety of bed, fatigue hits me. Minnie rewraps my leg after packing it with fresh poultice. I fall into a heavy slumber; a slumber that offers rest without worry, without retribution. The bed, funny bed at that, cradles me afloat. Oh, I am in a canoe on a very smooth waterway and carefree as a kingfisher who travels above the seamless brook waters.

STANDS LIKE A TREE VISITS

When I awakened there was someone else in Minnie's house. His voice rumbled like the trains in Halifax but I could not place him. With a few more words I recognized the wind and the rain in his voice. It was Stands Like a Tree. Would he scold me? Why would he be here at Minnie's house? He pulled a chair up to my bed. It screeched across the floor. With Minnie's assistance, I plumped pillows and sat up. Stands Like a Tree wore a fringed buckskin over a robe and breechcloth. He removed his buckskin and hung it on the back of the chair. His face looked like chiseled rock, a pronounced nose and thick, thick eye brows—so thick they reminded me of the brambles where we go berry-picking.

"You are a lucky youngster," he said. "You likely would have become food for the wolves or coyotes had I not heard your moaning." I shivered into my bones from his remark and clasped my hands.

Minnie, too, pulled up a chair. The fire from the hearth cast a warm glow over both of them. They looked like angels sitting there. I hated to admit it, but I felt extra special on occasion of his visit. Father would not take kindly to my situation though. He would probably think both Minnie and Stands Like a Tree were co-conspirators in my wrong-doing. Perhaps he would even forbid my ever seeing them again.

"I nearly passed you on that trail and would have had I not heard your moans," Stands Like a Tree said. "You could have easily died out there in the woods. There was a layer of snow over you as though you were part of a felled log. It is a good thing my hunting dog was with me upon return from council with the Mohawks. He wagged his tail with a force I will not forget. He, too, must have heard you."

He stopped speaking for a moment, as though lost to his thoughts. Stands Like a Tree stretched his arms in front of him and continued, "When my dog plowed his nose through snow he nudged you. You again let out a moan and I knew someone was in trouble."

A dead Ella would not please me—lips blue and permanently sealed. I would thank this man who carried me to the safety of Minnie's house, but first I hastened to explain myself lest he think me a thoughtless youth.

So, I implored him, "You do not know why I headed your way. I was searching for medicine for my mother. She was foremost on my mind. I thought you might know of a cure or your medicine man would help me find a cure. Your people know more about herbs than anyone in Nova Scotia." Minnie cast a look that said calm down, and admittedly I nearly rose off the bed in an attempt to explain my situation.

Stands Like a Tree cupped his hand underneath his chin. "There is a time to go forward in life and a time to remain still. When the weather is unpredictable the mood of the earth says stand still. There are spirits in the wind and you would be wise to listen to them more carefully."

"But I know nothing of your spirits. They do me little good. But sometimes, I must admit, they flutter across the land."

Hopefully my response had not sounded impertinent. Father has always said, "Ella, you have a most impertinent nature. Please quell your passions." To soften my words, I told Stands Like a Tree how deeply grateful I was that he found me and assured him that if there was any way to show my gratitude I would be most honored. Minnie quietly nodded and smiled.

"Remember what I told you that night on the ice?" he asked.

Not only did I recall that strange night when the owls flocked above us, their wings scratching across the sky, I also recalled the impression it made on me. Afterwards, I wanted to know more about those who lived amongst us. The magic of that night on the ice was profound. The possibility of my being made from the stars had puzzled me and for days I tried to glean meaning from Stands Like a Tree's words.

As though noticing a stupefied expression on my brow, Stands Like a Tree went on to tell me more about the secret of the stars. I marveled over his knowledge of the world.

"When we die we go to the stars. It is from the stars that we are reborn. Our Great Spirit is named Manitou but we also have many other spirits that inform our lives on earth. People born of the stars are always able to recognize others born from them. Most White People are not born of the stars—they are born from distant planets."

"How do you know this?"

"I know this from feeling. When I heard your voice a surge familiar as my own pounding blood ran through me. Voice is a direct line from the heart," he pondered for a moment before continuing. "If you listen for heart in a voice you must be prepared for disappointment. Few possess it. Even amongst our own People there are few who have come from elsewhere."

"There, now you know," Minnie said, rubbing her hands together in delight.

"Minnie, too, is from the stars," he added. "We have a gathering of stars right here in this room. We could even say, although it would be an exaggeration, we are an entire galaxy. Just the three of us."

Those words brought a smile upon my face and Stands Like a Tree smiled too, something he seldom did. His is a serious face, determination set in his jaw. Perhaps that is why his jaw is wooden-like and squared off. It is a jaw that walks ahead of him as though warning others to use caution. My face is heart-shaped, my chin forming a rounded u so my jaw, therefore, cannot walk ahead of me. For this, I am grateful. I will be a woman one day and would hate terribly to hold a stern countenance.

NEVER AGAIN WOULD I look at the stars in the same way. I would say nothing to my parents about the stars. There is much one is wise to keep to one's self. A spoken word has power and can change the course of events.

But Stands Like a Tree did not stop there. "I need to tell you something about the Mohawks. They will kill me at the first chance they get."

I shook my head. My father once said they were a fierce people and to be alert for trouble. Father said they carry fire in their bodies and are as light-footed as a falling leaf but that we were fortunate they have done no wrong to us or the villagers.

"The Mohawks sided, many years back, with the Protestants and the English. My people will not forgive them for that. Together, they exterminated a whole Micmac village on the Bay of Chaleur."

"But what does that have to do with you?" I asked.

"It has everything to do with me. I am alerting all the tribes in the area to be on the lookout for the Mohawks because they are moving our way. They know me as a message carrier and will slit my throat. They also know my reputation with a knife. Magic was given to me by a Micmac Medicine Man who showed me how to sharpen the knife's edge on a rock. The knife is hidden deep in the forest inside an oak burl and it holds considerable powers. No one else knows of its whereabouts."

Minnie then interjected, "They know I have befriended Stands Like a Tree so we must use extra caution. I never go to the outhouse at night or check on the chickens in the dark."

Frankly, the thought of something terrible happening to Minnie worried me. Her living alone and removed from town made me fear for her safety. A Mohawk could press his face to the window, watch her every move, and when she fell asleep, attack.

"Why don't you move into River John?" I asked, adding "Father has a sister who is looking for a boarder. You should take a room with her."

Minnie gave me a disapproving glance, shrugged her shoulders and said, "My home is right here and here is where I will remain. Stands Like a Tree checks on me every other day. Also, I pray for the Mohawks. The power of prayer keeps me safe." Minnie wiped her brow. Such talk made her sweat. There was such determination on her face that I feared she might keel over. "This is where my husband was granted our land, this is where we built our home, and I will not, not for anything, be removed."

By the tone of Minnie's voice I knew this was true. I also knew that danger was not far from her house. For that matter, it was never far from my parents' house or any of the villagers in town. Perhaps the most dangerous situations always resided in careless acts and I thought of my own foolishness striking out in bad weather in search for a cure for my mother. No, it is most easy to allow a foolish moment slip one up. It seduces one with excitement and promises of fulfillment until the unsuspecting person is charmed into compliance. A legtrap can be hidden underneath snow and stop one in her very tracks. One minute you think you are going someplace and the next minute you are snapped back into harsh reality.

Yet, despite those thoughts, I did not know then what lay ahead. A terrible mourning lurked in my future, and a terror that riveted my nerves and set my hands to many tasks.

GRIEF TIME

Father never did punish me for taking off on my own. When he picked me up at Minnie's, his only words on that long sleigh ride back to West Branch were, "I hear there were reasons you set your foot in danger. We will not discuss them at home. It is best your sisters hear nothing of your travails. The house is tied up in worry and we have no energy to discuss the motives behind your whereabouts. I have told Abbey and Cassie you have been lodging at Ernestine's. I urge you to say the same. But thank the good Lord you are alive and here beside me," and he gave my hand a little squeeze.

I said nothing in response. It was not a time to chat with Father. The horses seemed surly as they neighed, tossed their magnificent heads, billowy puffs of breath escaping their nostrils. The air was crisp, the light tinged in morning blue. I dreaded walking into the kitchen with no cure in my hands.

Father had fetched me so suddenly Stands Like a Tree had no time to search for a cure. And perhaps there was none, only hope on the doorstep of declining health. Hope was downcast, a ravaged soldier on the battlefield. Soon, we were all weary to a fine exhaustion, cleaning house, making meals and hauling in wood. Father busied himself in the shed making a pine coffin.

Mother died two days before Christmas and our house became sodden with tears. It was a depressing time. Hours before her death, my sisters became so contrary that I actually wished no sisters were ever given to me. They repeatedly sassed me. Father became distant as a rock lodged upon a precipice—cold and sullen. He said, "Let them be. Cassie and Abbey are just working off worry," so I said nothing to them.

To lay aside my sadness and anger, I knitted mittens not only for our family, but also for the poor families in town. I busied myself with purpose, knit socks and long flowing scarves. Knitting is like prayer, one loop equals one word. Each finished item then becomes the history of a particular prayer or hymn. Not that there was any certainty in positive results of either. A few days after our mother's death, everyone, for a short respite, was on their very best behavior. My sisters and I washed her with lilac soap. With a bone comb, I fluffed her hair in a lovely array that framed her face. She seemed relaxed in death. It was as though pain clarified her being and turned her pure. Her skin seemed ivory and pulled close to the bone. Blue veins threaded her forehead. Unfortunately, she would rest in the pine coffin at the graveside's stone mausoleum until spring time when burial was possible. And we would go through grieving twice as long because of a double goodbye.

"She looks like an angel," Abbey noted.

"Certainly our mother will be amongst the very best in heaven," Cassie replied, her eyes downcast, cheeks red from crying.

For me, there were no words except the words I said in secrecy to my Mother inside myself.

YOU WERE THE BEST MOTHER. *You made our home warm with love and tenderness. You were not quick to temper either, unlike Abbey who must be a generational throwback on some devilish side of the family. Your hands were silk when you stroked my brow to lay aside my fears. We called them the night tremors and you were slow to believe your first child was afraid of anything.*

How I loved to listen to your voice. It was a seasoned voice filled with thick mystery. I always told myself I would one day talk like you. I practiced and practiced out by the old apple tree where no one could hear me, but still my voice sounded like Ella and none other.

I imagined your voice having roots in moist, rich soil. I imagined flowers growing on a trellis inside your throat so that each word brushed against their sweetness before reaching your mouth. The very air we breathed was sweetened with the songs you sang. Oh, Mother, did I ever tell you which of those songs I loved best? If not, let me sing you this one:

Coulter's Candy
Ally, bally, ally bally bee,
Sittin' on yer mammy's knee
Greetin' for anither bawbee,
Tae buy mair Coulter's candy.
Ally. bally, ally, bally bee,
When you grow up you'll go to sea,
Makin' pennies for your daddy and me,
Tae buy mair Coulter's Candy.
Mammy gie me ma thrifty doon
Here's auld Coulter comin' roon
Wi' a basket on his croon
Selling Coulter's Candy.
Little Annie's greetin' tae
Sae whit can puir wee Mammy dae
But gie them a penny atween them twae
Tae buy mair Coulter's Candy.
Poor wee Jeannie's lookin' affa thin,
A rickle o' banes covered ower wi' skin,
Noo she's gettin' a double chin
Wi' sookin' Coulter's Candy.

(Meaning of unusual words:
bawbee=Once a silver six penny coin, in the days of Scottish coinage, now only a half-pennny.
trickle=heap)

But Mother, you have got no double chin. You were "A rickle o' bones covered ower wi' skin." I promise you this: if I were to one day have a child, I would sing that song to her and tell her that my mother is not just an angel in heaven—she was an angel on earth—an almost unheard of thing. But, if I become a writer, or a doctor, I will probably resist having a child. One cannot spread one's self too thin. You often reminded me of that when I set about too many tasks all at once, leaving items that needed to be mended idle upon the table. I am not sure about being a doctor though. Where would I go to school? What school admits girls? It is not fair. I live in a world that is made for men. Daughters cannot even inherit their father's land.

Another thing lest I forget. Say nothing, not even when you greet Father at that magnificent door leading into heaven, about the beaded eight point star I pressed into your hand. It was given to me by the Micmac, Stands Like a Tree. Please let that be our secret. I endowed it with a poem recited by me and written by Robert Burns. I kissed those words upon its surface, across even the prickly quills. It is to keep you safe, Mother. You might like to have something from earth up there amongst the stars, something to remind you of home in Nova Scotia where the green land and wildflowers bless the face of the earth and the water is nearly golden in the brooks.

Please, occasionally, look kindly down upon me as I will most certainly look up into the field of stars to find your face. If it takes me hundreds of nights, I will do so. When I find you, I will trace your smile with my finger and touch that finger lightly upon my heart.

Berries Black as Tar

The wind is the best thing about summer. It seems the trees are harp strings through which the breeze plays its finest music. No matter the strength of grief that attempts to overtake one, the clear-washed days of summer buoy one up and assure one that goodness rests at the center of the world. I think of Minnie, her resolute need to assist others in their time of travail and plan a visit to her at week's end. Dear Minnie, who so tenderly cared for me, will not be forgotten. She kept me warm, encouraged me to walk, and fed me the most delicious stews and coddled eggs.

SUMMER IN COLD COUNTRY is enjoyed more because it is so earned with all the miserable weather one endures. This part of the world breeds hardy souls. They have to be in order to get by. But the coldness makes for strong character. One cannot stand idle for long or a damp chill sets in. That makes for an industrious people.

"Cassie, wait up," I yell after my sister, who, for some reason beyond me, insists on flaunting her youth.

"Are you finding that you cannot keep up, Ella? Getting old, Ella? Pretty soon you will be an old woman," Cassie yells as she teases me.

"We shall see about that." I gather my dress lest I trip and break into a run, the berry basket swinging to and fro beside me.

I will show her. "You just wait, Cassie. I am no old woman."

"You are so old," Abbey, who insisted on spoiling our day with her presence, hollers my way. Father told her to accompany us because he has deliveries in town and needs to stock up on feed for the animals. He does not want her left alone at home.

Her words so annoy me that I break into a sweat and overtake Abbey. "Getting old, Abigail?" I say, passing her. "The heat wearing you out? You never were made of strong stamina."

"How dare you call me Abigail? I detest that name. Watch out, or I will pull every hair off your living head. "

"You will have to catch me first," I yell back at her. A good romp in the middle of a hot day sends sweat trickling between my breasts. It tickles as it slides downward.

Cassie's hair is golden and floats on a wave of air. I draw nearly close enough to reach out and tap her shoulder, but instead pass her, determined to outrun them both if it kills me. Suddenly I lose grasp of the berry basket and it tumbles into the grass.

That is when I am forced to stop running.

"Let us take the footbridge across the brook and see if we can make it to Fitzpatrick Mountain, at least the foot of it," Cassie says. "I love that place with its crowd of trees and birds."

"It is somewhat further than we told Father," I respond. "But why not? It is so pretty there mid-summer and there are the best berries there just west of the brook."

"I refuse to walk that far," Abbey announces, a pout set to her mouth, a grim, clenched- tooth look that reminds me of a dog spinning in to bite.

"Good, you can remain behind and if the Mohawks come they can take you and your mouth too."

"Not fair. We are not supposed to split up when we are out on our own."

"If you were not so blasted mean it would not be a problem. But you act like your hand's stuck in a hornet's nest ninety percent of the time."

"Perhaps we should ease up on her," Cassie says. "You never know what might be on her mind." Consoling Cassie always intervenes. "Besides, Mother said before she died that we should be good to one another. Now, we have this beautiful day open before us. What more could we possibly ask for?"

"Do you think you can make it to Fitzpatrick Mountain with us, Abbey?" I ask. "And, do you think you can continue to carry our picnic without stumbling or sputtering all the way there?"

Inside the basket we have chunks of sweet cheese, some thick, crusted bread and honey, plus three tart apples for dessert. We also have a little jar of creamy milk, drawn fresh from Malinda this morning, and six letters from Father to our mother when he was courting her that we plan to read over lunch.

"Suppose so, providing you keep from walking too fast, but not until you apologize, Ella, for calling me Abigail."

"Sorry."

You see, I did not attach an "I am" to it which means my "sorry" floats around in the air without an owner. Words without owners cannot count for much. Abbey will never recognize the importance of such an omission because she is exceedingly full of herself.

She looks pathetic beside me; her braids loose at the ends and her face mopped in sweat. Her eyes are cobalt blue and nearly burn straight through me. They remind me of a real hot fire similar to the ones Father made many years back when he was clearing our land for a patch of cow pasture.

Abbey's blouse's buttons have come undone and her apron is twisted backwards, the ties nearly touching her toes.

"You are a sorry sight," I tell her.

She shifts her apron round right and wipes her face on the sleeve of her blouse. As if there stirred no trouble between us, she suggests we pick wildflowers and wear little crowns of flowers on our heads. It puzzles me how quickly her mood changes. It is as though she were made of mercury.

The fields are full of Bunchberries, their stout white blossoms nodding in the breeze, Lady Slippers with their pink tongues, Asters and purple Lupine. It is the Lupine against the green, wild-grasses that stand out the most. We pick more wildflowers than we need, tossing the rejects aside and plunk ourselves down in the middle of the field while we make flower-crowns, tying the stems together to hold tight.

"How about we press the flowers into Father's new Bible when we return home," Cassie suggests. We all agree that is a splendid idea. It will give the book some character. The pages still smell of printer's ink.

Near the sloping hills, a great puff of smoke from McDonald's Wood Mill fills the air. Like boats adrift a timeless sea, the smoke lazily sails the sky. All around, the land is a beauty—glade upon glade of soft blowing grasses.

"Why not pass the crowns around and around and the first one that sees a bluebird keeps whichever crown lands in her hands?" Cassie says. When we focus on something else, the three of us get on quite nicely. Soon all three of us have crowns but we do not loiter for long when we have a fair distance between ourselves and the blackberries.

The worst thing about this outing is that insects thrive in the warm summer weather. Swarms of mosquitoes have no qualms whatsoever about coming out in direct sunlight. Even though we have rubbed ourselves with catnip and rosemary, they still drill into our skin, leaving us with huge welts.

I try with all my might not to scratch because it so enrages the poisons. It takes a mountain of discipline to keep from scratching a mountain of irritation. I turn my mind to the mouth watering berries we soon will pick. I imagine blackberry pie and preserves for warm bread fresh from the oven.

"Whatever happened between you and Billy O'Flannigan?" Abbey asks, her skirt brushing against mine. It strikes me as odd she brings this up.

"That is none of your business, Abbey," I reply.

"Well, I heard from Ernestine that you find him ill mannered on account of his speaking unkindly to a Micmac."

"And what else did pristine Ernestine tell you?"

"Please, no arguments," Cassie interjects.

But we act as though Cassie said nothing. Curiosity mounts with Abbey's question and I ponder her real motives.

"Nothing else, except she finds it strange such a little thing would so anger you."

"I do not have to account for my actions. I simply do not like Billy anymore. That is it, simple and true."

"Then you should not mind he has asked me to the barn dance in August. I have wanted to tell you for some time." Her face glows with satisfaction—she fairly drools with pride. Needles of anger flare in my eyes. I should have known Abbey's questions would lead to a surprise. But I slough it off with, "I hope you have a good time. You are meant for each other."

"What do you mean by that?" she asks.

To further myself from my source of irritation, I walk much faster. Cassie calls after me to slow down.

Fitzpatrick Mountain is straight ahead and we walk underneath an arbor of the most splendid birch trees, bits of bark peeling back from them like tiny wings. The smell of the earth, due to the light and porous quality of the soil, is sweet. I inhale deeply as though smell could plant this very soil inside me. Often, as a child, I thought that if I swallowed an apple seed I might grow an apple tree inside me. I imagined it growing roots, a trunk and splendid branches with bright apples. With soil like this I could have grown anything inside me. I wonder when childish thoughts dry up and all of us begin to carry the weight of impending adulthood.

Slivers of silver light spark the sumacs and woody pines. They drip in silver. The sun breaks through in planks of light. A tightly woven forest such as this holds a sense of mystery. Soon we three are walking in unison as though there was never room for rancor.

"What if we see a moose?" Cassie asks.

"Head for a sturdy tree and climb like the devil is in your bloomers," I tell her.

"What if we happen upon the Mohawks?" Abbey wonders aloud.

"We best hope we never come across them. Fie, Fie to mention such a possibility."

The prospect of berries quickly replaces fear. But I must admit, the thought of the Mohawks entered my mind too. But no, they would be down by the shores at this time of year, casting for fish, or rowing their nets out to then haul back when they were laden with catch

I lesson myself on what to do should we come across them: act brave, do not cower and especially do nothing to accelerate their mood. Father shared that with us and he certainly has experienced their nature on more than one occasion.

"Look at the huge skunk cabbages down by the creek," Cassie points out.

Sure enough, there is a tribe of them along the muddy banks. Their centers host flutes of a single, yellow flower, a flower that's nearly as long as their green velvety leaves. Back home, I sometimes run a skunk cabbage leaf across my face—in that moment I am truly loved by the earth.

Ahead, we spot a tangle of berry bushes and break out in laughter.

Abbey sings out, "I was skeery and bashful at first and then guess what?"

We had no idea what she was talking about. Also, exuberance is not something normally thought of when I think of Abbey, but human nature is strange. Just when I have someone's nature nailed in place he or she startles me. As Abbey repeats those lines I join in, and Cassie too, and we quickly switch to something different, a Scottish song the three of us often sing because it seems like a good picking song, *Little Matha Grove*:

> `Twas on a day, a high holiday
> *The best day of the year,*
> *When little Matha Grove he went to church*
> *The holy word to hear.*
> *Some came in diamonds of gold,*
> *And some came in in pearls,*
> *And among them all was little Matha Grove*
> *The handsomest of them all.*

We have become a regular committee of scrambled brains in our silliness and we laugh until I think I will pee. We sing and pick, pick and sing. Our fingers quickly dart in and out of the blackberry

bushes. Little laps of sunlight wash over us. There are fewer mosquitoes than before and that makes for a better mood. Occasionally, one
of us yelps out from thorny jabs.

Abbey has stopped telling me about Billy's invitation and to
tell the truth I really care little if she goes with him. He has passed
through my being like rain water through a leaky barrel. That night
on the ice fixed that. Afterwards, I decided Billy was not of the right
temperament for a girl with a poetic nature. No, I need no man. I
have my dreams and they are the keenest gentlemen in all of Nova
Scotia. They do not argue with me, they do not say I have to be this
or that, but they do request I live up to my potential. So, I will become a disciple to my dreams. Even so, there is one, as of late, who
surfaces in my thoughts and it troubles me.

HOW TASTY IS A FLAKEY PIECE of bread with honey and cheese.
We spread an old horse blanket on the ground and sit and partake
of our lunch. Abbey gobbles the food like she has not eaten in years,
whereas Cassie, the golden one, daintily breaks small pieces of crust,
dabs them in honey, and slowly chews as though pondering some
great event in her life. We have spread Father's yellowish letters in the
center of our picnic area and plan to take turns reading them aloud
after lunch. The envelopes are soft as velvet.

Our berry basket is brimming over with blackberries, a few tufts
of leaves interspersed here and there as well as tiny bugs who must
find a single berry as big as a small world.

There is such satisfaction in gathering berries. That is how I feel
working with words. I am a word picker. Whole worlds come alive
in the basket of my life. More and more my thoughts turn toward
becoming a writer. It somehow seems less complicated. But I must
wait and see. One should not close options too soon.

Little kites of dust motes float in the air and when the sun hits
just right they sparkle with silver. The day is most divine. The earth
has never known a single bad thing on a day like this. No bloodshed,
no colonists taking over land that originally belonged to others, no
British making war, no Scottish landlords throwing people out of

Scotland in the Great Clearances—eager to consolidate small properties into profitable sheep farms, and no accidents of falling trees on settlers like what happened last year to Timothy Hardy. He died when a tree struck him, a branch embedded in his chest.

First there was a loud snap and then he was pinned underneath a pine. No circle of men could lift that tree, and Father, not known for cursing, was reported to have said such profanity it could not be repeated. He supposedly repented his words later that week at church.

We were aghast when we heard of his intemperance.

ABBEY PICKS OUT ONE of the yellow creased letters and starts quietly reading it aloud—the paper soft as fuzzy catkins found on Aspen Poplars:

Dearest Martha,

Pardon me for bulging your postal way box with my incessant writings, but I have been granted a parcel of crown land, good land I might add. There are, in all, one hundred acres. I fancy we can build a house, some out-buildings and level land for a pasture. There are maple trees to tap and we will have our very own maple syrup. There is much work to be done. So much, it is nearly overwhelming. The land is thick with trees and goodly space must be cleared for building and such, as well as for planting a vegetable garden.

I know you are caring for your grandfather and hoped to stay on in Halifax until he regained his health. But I bid you come, my dear girl, so we can build upon our future.

You promised you would consent to my proposal of...

AND THEN THEY CAME

First there was a subtle rustling of leaves. We thought them wind-swept. Alarm sealed Abbey's lips from reading out loud and shock raced through her eyes quicker than bolts of lightning. Waves of danger fairly rippled through the air. Not one of us spoke. Blood pounded furiously through my temples, my hands twisted in a knot. I stared through the trees but nothing seemed amiss. Still, the leaves rustled some distance away as though in warning.

Robins that previously perched on the birch limbs were gone, as were the wrens and nuthatches. Even squirrels disappeared. Both seemed a forewarning. I had seen that before when certain wild animals encroached upon our properties, especially when the sheep were lambing—birds took off in absolute fright.

No quiet is more pronounced than fear's quiet. A silence fell darker than midnight. I knew not what to do. Here we were seated on the ground, blackberry bushes to one side and a thicket of trees to the other. Certainly we would be seen if a marauding tribe or French hunters passed through. What devilish nature lay before us? I brought my forefinger to my lips to signal hush, my sisters looking at me in alarm. There was simply nowhere to go or time to take cover.

Time did not move, yet there was movement in the near distance. There were no voices, only the scuffle of someone or something making its way through the forest. Could it be an animal? An animal, or so it seemed, would move in a more erratic manner, stop to forage on trees and ferns. There was purpose in what I heard. And then they came. First one Mohawk, another and another and another.

They were bare-chested and bronze. Each carried something in their hands. It looked like a stick, but I suspected it was no stick—more like a strike-you-dead club. Their heads were shaved while a tuft on top of their heads was worked into a crest of hair that ran from forehead to the backs of their heads and was dyed a brilliant red. Father called them warrior's roaches after we found some on the ground. They were made of porcupine hair, moose hair or deer's tail hair. The wiry animal hair is then threaded through their own tufts of hair to stiffen it so that it stands straight up on their heads. There was something beautiful, though strangely startling in how they looked.

If purpose has thrust, they certainly bore that thrust with pride as they bolted forward, one following the other. I could not help but think this was their land and that it would always be their land. We Scottish were just visitors.

But what was I thinking at such a time? Fear smells like brackish water. It ravaged my nostrils, fairly burning the little hairs in my nose. We each cast a glance at one another without moving our heads, Cassie's eyes sparked with fright. Remain still our eyes ordered each other. We were inert as quarry marble. One of them broke through the curtain of leaves to directly face us. His eyes were fierce. His chest was wide, not an ounce of fat.

I could not figure whether to stand or remain still, but chose the latter. *Wait. Wait until he does something.* Neither of my sisters had the bad judgment to get up and break into a run. Certainly, I was going nowhere. The Mohawk edged right up to the rim of our tablecloth, lorded his chest over us. The others halted on the upper path that led down to our berry bounty. The nearby man scooped down over us, stuck his finger in the honey jar and smacked his lips. For fear he might bump into me, I crouched sideways from my seated position. I was barely breathing, my heart leapt like a mad man jailed for the first time.

Oh, please, please, keep us safe dear Lord. I am sorry for all the wrong done by my person. I repent all my bad deeds, as do my sisters. Surely, I can speak for them as the eldest. I know their nature completely, and my own less so. Kindly do not think me presumptuous. If

we make it through this we can make it through anything. Never again
will we chance an outing this far from home.

Then the strangest thing happened. He grabbed the jar of honey
and disappeared into the canopy of leaves. We did not speak. We
dared no words. Breathless and stunned we looked at one another.
I whispered, "Do not move." We sat for several deafening moments
before I stood, looked around to insure they indeed were gone.

"All is clear." But no sooner were those words spoken when a realization struck me. They were headed toward our place, or Minnie's,
or they were out to hunt down Stands Like a Tree. With growing
surety, I believed the real danger ahead. "We must not tarry. Gather
your things Abbey and Cassie."

Cassie was white as the sheets on Father's bed and with lackluster
effort she helped pick up. Abbey and I folded the blanket. Cassie said
she felt ill and by the looks of her she would topple over any moment.
I practically forced a cup of milk down her to fortify what strength
remained.

"We have been spared," Abbey said. "What is the hurry?"

I snapped back, "For a varmint's sake, will you listen and do as
told?"

She screwed her face up like the headmaster, Hector Adams. They
would do well together, but unfortunately Hector is not the marry-
ing type and he is much older. No woman, I suspect could stand to
live with him. I tell my sisters we are not entirely out of danger as we
walk back at a good clip. It is never as fun to head home as it is to
head out and my feet have lost their earlier urgency.

We keep a look out for further trouble. My eyes grow keener.
Sometimes seeing is not really seeing unless you are completely settled into seeing. Sitting on my bed and looking out the window gives
me real seeing. And then of course there is the inner seeing which I
call speculative and contemplative.

As the sun drops, the trees take on a somewhat sinister look. I
scoop up several moose stones. Moose swallow small stones to aid
in digestion and the stones end up in one of their two stomachs before they pass them. They are round and polished like gems. Into my

pocket I drop them for good luck. If not luck, they will become worry stones. A stone, under the right conditions, can become a saint of softness.

As we return home, I cast piercing glances every which way but notice nothing. I must, as soon as possible get to Minnie's and let her know my worst fears. Father will surely take me to her place, providing he is not still miffed at her for stowing me away after my snowy escapade. But he should be thankful that someone took such good care of his daughter at a time when others were preoccupied with Mother. Stands Like a Tree must be warned too, but I shall not mention that to Father for fear he would admonish me. I am certain he does not want his name uttered in our home. No, I suspect he worries over my impulsiveness.

In the distance I spot our cows. We have two milking cows out grazing and Malinda, the one I named, is my favorite. She has huge black patches, the rest of her white, and the kindest eyes. Cows never seem to hurry. They are like huge boulders that know their place. Perhaps I do not know my place. Perhaps, instead of running off to see Minnie and Stands Like a Tree, I should check if Father has some work for me.

People of the Flint
& a Trip Into Town

A s we near the house we see Father unhitch the horses and walk them to the pen. He steps inside the barn to check on Lucinda, our best Holstein, who is due to calf and rushes back out, his face anxious. Abbey runs ahead of Cassie to tell him of our experience. This angers me because I wanted to relay the news about the Mohawks myself, but he pays little heed to Abbey's idle chatter, a frown raked across his brow.

Instead, he quickly unloads feed as she sputters on about what we saw, her hands jabbing the air. He looks to me for confirmation and I nod. His face gives little away, but the speed with which he unpacks his supplies tells me something different. Without a single word, Father hauls the sacks to the barn and secures the door with a quick slide of the latch.

"Enough prattle, daughters. We are going to ride into town." Trouble spreads across his face like a sea gathering to storm. "Abbey, get me the horses to hitch. Cassie, you check the house and make sure we have no candles going and that the grate is on the cook stove. Also, bring my leather pouch."

What so provokes Father that he will not tell what is on his mind? It must have something to do with the Mohawks. This is not the first time he has gone tight-lipped. The last day of Mother's life, she in such pain, he became nearly paralyzed. Each scream, "Oh, God take me, please," tightened the grip of his hands until his knuckles were white.

"Death is an ugly business," he later told the doctor.

We hustle, board the wagon and soon we are bound for town. I sit up front with Father. He asks me to keep an eye out, not for Mohawk trouble but for new ruts from the last summer storm of the year. Bad ruts are known to tip a wagon, or bust the wagon's wheel-lockings.

I cannot bear the mystery of his silence, worry pushes my thoughts against my skull until they rattle. "Father, do you think the Mohawks are a danger to us? Is that why we are headed to town?" I ask.

He looks scruffy in the dim light. "No, we are headed to town because Lucinda is calving and the calf is stuck. I must call on Joseph for help providing he is not off to Halifax. We will fetch him back with us. I need strong hands and calving ropes to pull this one. I cannot afford the loss of either the mother or the calf."

My sisters let out a sigh behind me. Surely they thought we were escaping some horrific danger, but I think there is uncertainty in the air and it has nothing to do with our animals. I twist and untwist my hands. The coming night feels damp across my cheeks, the air more humid.

"Are you at all worried about our having seen the Mohawks?"

"Not really. They are not out to harm us. They have more trouble with the Micmacs."

"But Father, I thought you always told us to keep a keen eye out for them. Why?"

"It is wise to know where migratory people are. You might liken it to knowing when new neighbors come to roost in these parts. Besides, if there is unrest we would have heard by now. The village fathers keep track of such things."

"Would you drop me off so I can tell Minnie what we saw? I fear she might be in danger."

Those words, spoken at the wrong moment, so anger Father he nearly drops the reins. If he ever intended to slap me it is right about now. He gathers the reins in one hand and raises his hand in front of me. I scrunch down expecting a slap, but he soon drops his hand. He has never struck one of us, but I truly feared in that moment he was too close to anger. Instead, he casts a fearful glance at me before saying, "Ella, do you not have better sense than bring such a subject up now? Me, sick with worry over the calf yet born and its mother. You, of all people, know how much we rely on our farm animals."

I am sickened unto my soul for my impetuous nature. Surely, I should have waited. But worry rages within my breast. How will Minnie protect herself if the Mohawks are after her? How will Stands Like a Tree warn his people?

Father starts coughing and asks for some black currant lozenges from his travel pack. I fish around and find a lozenge which I dutifully pass him.

"I nearly lost control," Father shamefully says. "Will you forgive me, Ella?"

Not only do I forgive him, I also apologize for asking him about taking me to Minnie's house. Inside myself though, I shiver with concern. As diversion, I ask questions about the Mohawks.

"Father, you have, upon occasion, met with the Mohawks, especially when the Micmacs and townsfolk called forth a meeting to discuss properties. Do you think they were scouting for trouble?"

"Could be they are just out to trade corn or furs with their neighbors. You said they wore roach headdresses?"

"Yes, and some had paint on their faces."

Oh, they were most frightful," Abbey pipes up from the back of the wagon.

"Still, I am not concerned. No word has spread of any trouble. You know those moccasins I wear? They were given to me by a wizened, old Mohawk who did some water dowsing for us when we cleared and built our house. Nicest man I ever met. He told me stories about The People of the Flint. Unfortunately, many of his people died off from European diseases. Many of the Mohawks, and rightfully so, consider us nearly poisonous."

In the distance, with encroaching night, an owl screeched. The hair on the back of my neck rose. The wagon rattled as we traveled over the wooden bridge leading into River John. It sounded like cannons going off. Houses were lit with kerosene lamps; a warm glow flickering in the windows. Never did a house seem more warm and inviting than evening, or so I have always found. Father pulled into a drive, passed me the reins and jumped down from the wagon.

"You wait while I fetch him, providing he is home." Father took his coin pouch with him and disappeared. We heard him knock on the door. The only other sounds were crickets strumming the air. The moon was slowly edging up. By the time we get back it will be overhead the barn. I inhaled deeply as though air itself could wash my body of fear.

THE BIRTHING OF TWINS

Lucinda did not have one calf. She birthed two: a bull and a heifer. The male came first and was much larger. Lucinda lay on a freshly piled nest of hay exhausted, belly heaving in contractions. Joseph looped the calving ropes around the calf's two front legs and he and Father pulled. But first, Joseph determined which way the calf was facing and then repositioned its head. Abbey and I held lanterns so the men could see. We also left the barn doors open to let the moonlight in. It cast a warm glow that made the hay golden.

The barn smelled of hay and cows and sheep. Every so often Lucinda let out a mournful moo, tossed her head to and fro. It cannot be easy being a cow in the middle of birth, I thought. Without words, how do cows know what their own bodies are up to? This proved most puzzling. I set my lantern on a hook and walked over to her, reached down and petted her head and she let out another moo, her long, silky eye-lashes framed her eyes. I resisted the temptation to kiss her forehead.

As soon as the forelegs and nose appeared, Joseph gave the calf's tongue a pinch. "Good," he said. "The tongue retracted. That is just what we want from a healthy animal. Once the tongue grows yellowish things get more complicated." He also tickled its nose with a hay piece because that stimulates breathing.

I asked him, "What is the most important thing when helping a cow calf?"

Joseph stopped pulling on the rope, ran a hand through his beard and said, "Making sure you never yank. You have to have patience with these animals. They have keen instincts and can, right away, read a fellow. You must avoid pulling on the calf's head too."

Abbey could not resist opening her mouth to say something stupid. "Ella, why not give him a hand?" A big smirk on her face so irritated me that I wanted to say something mean, but instead clenched my fist. You are the oldest, I told myself. You must set a good example. It would not be kind to enter into disagreement in front of Father's helper. "We can handle things quite fine, Abbey." Father, thank goodness, knows Abbey's nature. "Ella, fetch that lantern. Hold it close so we can see. No more mollycoddling, Lucinda. Animals have been birthing for centuries," Father instructed.

I moved near Joseph, although we girls called him Sir. He smelled of tobacco and a pipe stuck out from his shirt pocket.

"Pull the calf in a steady motion during contractions," Joseph added. "You also want to make certain the legs are in the birth canal, and not caught up on the pubic bone. Many a calf is lost on account of such things."

Through the haze of night I caught Abbey's eye. She was lost to her own thoughts. Most probably she was thinking about the barn dance with Billy.

With a few more tugs, the male calf rested contentedly in the hay. Lucinda turned to check on him. The second calf, a surprise, was much smaller and came on its own down the birth canal. This happened so quickly we were taken off guard and most thankful things were not more complicated. Father said afterwards that we got two for the price of one.

The afterbirth flushed out and Lucinda lifted the great heft of her weight to stand and turn so that she faced her calves. Softly, even tenderly she toweled them clean with her long tongue. I had been so absorbed in the calving that I nearly forgot about the Mohawks. Oh, Minnie, that I could but warn you.

A Newcomer

The window weeps with rain, a soggy cloak of water on the land. Much has changed in our lives and not for the better. Father has remarried, our mother buried only five months. A man cannot be without a woman in these parts. There is simply too much to be done. My sisters and I tried to council him and for weeks we threw ourselves into cleaning and cooking thereby attempting to prove we were perfectly capable of handling all household matters. But he resisted our attempts and said daughters need a mother. I explained we had one perfectly good mother and that the impression she made upon us would last a lifetime. We needed no other.

So there is a newcomer in our lives. She is the Widow Applegate, from Toney River. Her smile is quick, her look deadly. She knows nothing of mothering as she has had no children of her own. I imagine her womb as dour as her face—nothing good could come from it. She has a mole to the side of her nose. It nearly overtakes her face. Sometimes I think the mole a piece of dirt and reach out to wipe it off. Then I remember her biting words, how she is perfectly capable of reducing a young woman to either tears or to a sweltering rage. Just last week she caused Abbey, who is a bit of a problem, days of wasting in bed.

"Child, the devil is in you," her finger pointing at Abbey. "Fire and brimstone is what you will reap. When the devil is in you you must not leave the house or he will grab you and tear your heart out. You must hang a twig of spruce directly over your bed. The devil fears spruce above all other things. You best hold steadfastness to Christ and His Church so fetch your Bible and read it." The Widow paused and continued her tirade. " And you will not attend the dance this week in River John. I forbid you to ask again. Is that understood between us?" She shook her finger underneath Abbey's nose.

Unfortunately, Abbey's scolding was not enough to quell her fire. Saturdays, in preparation for the Sabbath, we take turns soaking in the big tub hauled in from the barn and set in the middle of the kitchen floor which is made of river-stone. The flooring has a large drain with piping that leads far from the house. We heat kettle after kettle on the stove and pour it into the tub. After the Widow and Father have bathed, I am next, being the oldest. We add hot water from the stove as the tub water grows cold. At the end of our bathing, which requires an entire Saturday evening, we slowly dump the water in one huge wave. This both empties the tub and cleans the floor as well. But Abbey, eager to be done with it, spilled out so much water it lapped its way into the bedrooms creating a disaster.

The Widow yelled at Abbey for this unfortunate turn of events, "For this, you will render your small savings to me and I will use it for the church collection. Patience. Do you think you can remember patience in the future? If this happens again you will not be allowed to attend Sabbath with us. Instead, you will remain here and scrub the house clean. Is that understood?"

On Sabbath Day the Widow is extremely strict. We are not allowed a snicker, giggle or idle chatter. "No spiritedness on this day," she warns. We must sit for four hours in church. Two hours for the morning sermon and after a lunch break two more hours. Heaven forbid one of us should nod off, unable to survive the endless drone of Pastor Smith as he extols the Bible's virtues. His sermons lack vitality and as the air inside the church swells with all the villagers, stuffiness floats across the room. We are made to stand an hour in the corner upon return from church should one of us tilt towards sleep. The Widow's eyes tuck to our backs.

The Widow's former husband, Mr. Applegate, died of a heart attack. He worked at Nolan's Shipyard on the saw crew, a rowdy group, and was said to be a heavy fellow prone to imbibing too much prohibited whiskey and too many sweets. I suppose he had to build an armor of fat around himself to deflect the arrows from his wife's mouth. One day he walked off the job, sat by the waterfront and downed two flasks of fire-water. They say a bull moose chased him and he being so big was unable to get away. But the moose did not take him down; instead, his faulty heart killed him. The dock workers saw him lying flat on his face when they went to fetch him. They also saw moose tracks.

"Yes, ma'am," Abbey replied to the window's earlier question, a look of pure hatred in her eyes. I never, in all my life, witnessed such a cold glare.

Sometimes I feel Abbey has a side of her that could turn for the bad. As much as I do not like the Widow Applegate, as much as I fear her cranky nature, the importance of obeying one's elders is indelibly impressed upon my person. Or perhaps that is not quite true. Perhaps I am too close to myself for any objectivity. After all, who is the one who wandered astray on a long trek, unbeknownst to her parents?

Abbey could have heart trouble in the future given her obstinacy. We have heard that if you push hard enough at something your heart will give out. I take a heaping spoonful of apple vinegar and honey each day to keep my heart fit as a fiddle. Have not I, too, already disobeyed the Widow Applegate by checking on Minnie each week? And did I not find my way, unbeknownst to Father, into River John soon after the calves were born and before he remarried?

Oh, yes, indeed, I rode in with our neighbors the MacKays who kindly dropped me off at their store in town and I walked straight to Minnie's.

Home of Flesh

"Come on in child. What's on your mind?" asked Minnie. She was making jam and sweat sprinkled little raindrops onto her apron. Coils of hair curled at her neck, and they hung like stems of wilted flowers. Her kitchen smelled delicious. Everything about Minnie's house smelled like a baker's shop. Sunshine set the room ablaze. A pitchfork stood in the corner near the door. Minnie, undoubtedly, was putting hay aside before she started in on the jam. On her table was a bottle filled with fresh picked sunflowers; they insolently poked the air with their yellow petals and little insects flitted above the bouquet as though bugs, too, have tribal gatherings.

"Did you hear the Mohawks were up on Fitzpatrick Mountain?" I asked. Minnie licked the jam spoon and set it aside in the dish basin. "Yes, Stands Like a Tree told me they were around. But we have not had a spot of trouble in months and I anticipate none."

"But, Minnie, they were fearsome. One of the men grabbed a jar of honey from my sisters and me. They wore hair roaches and some were painted red. They reminded me of red-headed woodpeckers." "Did you not notice there were young boys with them?"

"No, I never saw the boys. I believe there were none."

"Well, my lass you are wrong. Stands Like a Tree said they were training their youngsters, that is all. They take their sons into the wild when they are quite young. You certainly know that. Sometimes they leave them in the wilderness to fend for themselves. It makes a man out of them, or so is their belief." She turned her attention back to sealing the jam jars with paraffin and she tells me that a Scottish man first made paraffin from shale.

"It is possible they had children in tow and that we never saw them through the bushes and veil of trees. But I truly felt they were on a sinister mission." I stopped talking for a moment and fished my hankie from my pocket to wipe my brow. "A thousand drums beat in my chest, Minnie, until they finally passed. It was quite terrifying, especially when one Mohawk broke from the trail and thieved our honey."

"Ella, he thieved nothing. All things nature made are for all. That is the law of the land here in Nova Scotia. Do you not recall stories of our first people that landed here, how everyone shared? The Micmacs, in particular, taught us much of what we know about survival." With no obvious concern regarding the Mohawk event Minnie asks, "How is your father doing with the widow Applegate? I heard he remarried." "He is doing fine. Only, we, his children, are not. The Widow carries a snake's venom in her body. My sisters and I do not get on with her. Honestly, Minnie, I have tried with all my might, but the woman treats us like we are very small children. When she first arrived at our house we made mincemeat fold-ups, quince cookies and set out Mother's best teapot from Scotland—all to welcome her but to no avail. She directly asked we immediately put such frivolous things back in the dish cabinet. Did we not think such extravagance foolish?"

"That is not very charitable," Minnie says as she again licks jam from her fingers. Tenderly, she caps each jar with little cloths given her by the Woman's Charity Society, leftovers from their church lawn sale. "Here is a jar for you to take back home. Let me know if the Widow likes my jam."

Minnie heads for the privy while I lick clean the pan. The jam slowly slides down my throat and I so savor that moment. Taste can sometimes remind us there is much sweetness in the world. No matter the sadness of loss, the travails visited upon one, there is always a moment of beauty in each day.

"Unbutton your eyes," I say to myself, "take notice of the world." That reminder sometimes tenders me sight of a cardinal, a doe and her fawn scampering across Father's landholding, or even an early evening sky painted with stretches of whimsical clouds. Water from the hand pump swirls around in the pan and as I am about to scrub it clean a most startled scream rises from the privy. I rush outside and swing open the door. There is Minnie standing on the wooden seat straddled above the hole, her dress pulled to her knees, her socks fallen at her ankles, one foot on the left board, another on the right.

"Watch out, Ella, there is a rattler in here big as my rake. Be careful. Go fetch the pitchfork and direct the rattlesnake towards the door. Hurry child. I fear he will thrust his poison upon me."

Without a moment's thought, I race to the house and grab the pitchfork, returning with the force of a gale off the Northumberland Straits. "It will be fine, Minnie. If I have to, I will pin it with one of the tines." But the thought of actually puncturing the snake's scaly skin causes goose bumps to rise on my arm. I have heard tell that the rattles make such a whishing sound that one never forgets the crispness of their papery rattle. Henceforth, great caution must be employed. By now, Minnie is visibly upset, knees shaking, face contorted. I fear she will fall from her perch. Cautiously, I run the pitchfork in the direction of the snake huddled in the corner. Should I attempt to reach in back of it and rake it forward, or should I attempt, ever so gently, to ply from the center of its coiled body until it comes undone and rests in a straight line? *Oh, foolish girl,* I tell myself, *would it, quite alive, remain in a straight line?*

I slowly wiggle the pitchfork in back of the beast and the moment I do so the terrible hissing of the rattles makes me lurch back. My body feels caught in its grip.

I am ever so mindful of Minnie, the closeness of the snake, the direction it could strike from. All the serpent must do is rise and face her. Minnie is hanging on to her dress as though mere material could steady her. Her face is frozen in one single expression of terror, her eyes closed.

"Minnie, let go of your dress and apron. It covers your legs and if the snake strikes that is where the beast will sink its ugly fangs. Keep your hands high." For a moment, I gather my wits and continue, "Snakes cannot bite through clothes." That belief, real or not, renders small comfort.

Fortunately, she does as I say, but she is so wobbly straddled atop the seat's hole I fear she will tumble from there straight onto the snake's back and startle it into striking her.

Dark marks run down the skin of the animal. Its sinuous body coils and uncoils. I lean into the pitchfork momentarily for support, the tines stuck into the wooden floor, and with a short reprieve, I hope to gain courage and move forward and pierce the coiled thing with the pitchfork. But first, I search outside for stones to toss for distraction.

The Bible holds good lessons on snakes but no instructions whatsoever for me at this murderous moment. *When God found out that the serpent had deceived Eve, He cursed him and commanded him to crawl on his belly. Eat of the apple and you will fall from grace.* I think no animal is mentioned or alluded to more than snakes in the Bible, and for good reason. They surely must represent all evil and are the designee of danger and downfall. The first stone makes no visible impression on the beast as it slithers to the other corner, while the next stone causes the rattler to rear, its head darting about in a strange, mesmerizing dance. The stone fails to strike it and only provokes the snake to glide to another spot.

With great caution I decide to levy the tines gently underneath the rattler, lift it and toss it outside, but the animal will have no such thing and slithers across the floor into the corner where the first stone hit. He is dangerously close to Minnie who screams, "Pierce it in its heart. Pierce it in its heart. Hurry, Ella, or my legs will give way," her gray hair coming undone from its bun. Minnie becomes white as the talcum powders women use after their baths.

I lift the pitchfork as though it were a gun, take aim at the snake's venom filled head and slam down the tines with no luck whatsoever. It is as though the serpent has sway over the metal forces of the tines, its eyes devious as a daemon.

Fearful, I am most fearful. It is a terrifying thing, the power of such an animal. Fright smells like gunpowder, my knees wobbly.

Once more I take aim and strike only empty floorboards. Stubborn pitchfork, stupid situation and aimless girl who cannot for the sake of her dear friend strike right.

Minnie veers forward. I must move fast. With the force of my entire being, I slam the pitchfork just below the snake's head, its tiny tongue lapping discontent. Pinned, the serpent is finally pinned. Its rattles, like a child's toy, shake in the air. But what to do now that it is pinned?

"Do not loosen your hold, Ella."

Minnie turns sideways and uses the wall for support as she steps down, ever cautious of the snake's whereabouts and scuttles from the privy, shaken unto her very heart. "I must sit. I cannot stand a minute more." She finds a stump to rest upon, her breathing deep, but with considerable relief.

"Use caution, child. That creature must be one of those swamp snakes the men folks tell about when they are lumbering and hauling wood. I think they are called Massasauga Rattlesnakes, seldom seen in these parts."

Oh, what am I to do with the snake now nailed by the tines, but very much alive and lunging back and forth?

Pierced, through and through, am I to scoot it out the door by dragging it forward? Quite likely it will live. I have heard Father tell of a snake's uncanny nature, how they can heal what would otherwise remain broken in humans. That must be the miracle of snakes. They live so close to the earth they must have been the earth's very first children. But back to the beast itself that stares at me with an uncanny eye.

The tines are not straight through the head, only below where the neck might be, or so I presume not being an expert on snakes. I carefully drag it forward and step back with each draw. It winds and unwinds in a rage. It is, at last, by the doorway and I must drop it down onto the plank step. Quickly, ever so quickly the creature is raked forward. With great tenderness now, lest I further hurt it, I attempt to disentangle the snake free from the tines. With a brisk shake of the pitchfork the snake is finally set free and flees under the blackberry bushes. It will, undoubtedly, slither as fast as it is able until it finds shelter in swamp milkweed.

"You did right, Ella. For a moment I was worried the creature would strike you. What an eventful day. Let us sip tea." Minnie stands, shakes out her cotton dress and apron as though they were somehow harmed by the snake's presence. She says, "I will open my very best London tin of tea sent to me by my sister in Saskatchewan. Let us lay out some shortbread cookies too. There must be celebration for your standing up to the beast."

I tell her to always close the privy's door. "That is how the snake got in, Minnie. You must not air your privy in summer when snakes hunt for rodents. Even the Widow Applegate, my stepmother, has warned me to always shut the door when we leave. Sometimes, though, admittedly, I leave it ajar so that the pesky flies and mosquitoes have more room to fan their wings and are less likely to feed on me. Also, there is a beautiful view with the door open, the lovely trees fanning their wings in the breeze. But, in the future Minnie, lest you cause me great concern, please keep the door shut."

"Go easy on the Widow Applegate," Minnie urges. "People are duel natured and I bank my money she has another side to her that is quite wonderful."

Minnie's eyes remind me of all the goodness banked in this world. They are eyes that warmly hold you in their sight and they seem to say, "You are the most splendid thing on earth." They are eyes that convey both trust and truth—old eyes that do not carry an ounce of pretense; eyes that invite you in to sit upon the soul.

There is no more special place on earth than to be a guest of someone's heart.

"I will try." Not that I really believed Minnie's words about the Widow, but when it seemed the world was pulled apart by opposing factors, such as Abbey's running off with Billy, Father shamed unto the core, I discovered the wisdom of Minnie's words.

Abbey Brings Shame upon the Family

Upon my soul, I am Ella, and none other. Because of that, it is with some restraint I tell you of Abbey's dalliance, especially given more serious things to come that held not a hint at the time of Great Shame. Had there been advance notice of what was about to befall Abbey, I would have solicited advice from my sister Cassie or my aunt. But life does not forewarn. If it did, we might not have the forbearance to move forward. No, there must be mystery at the center of the world or we would have no sense of awe looking upon the stars at night, no courage to make our way further into the days ahead.

But back to the subject at hand. Abbey and Billy planned to attend a barn-raising in Tatamagouche and were to stay the night at Aunt Kathleen's. Dear Aunt Kathleen who is the picture of endless patience, and who has become greatly saddened since our Mother's death, offered to host the two. She has always been my favorite relative. Not a bad word about a soul spills from her lips. She too, is widowed, her children off to Halifax where there is more opportunity for employment.

So the Widow Applegate and Aunt Kathleen gave great consideration to ensure all was proper and that the two, my sister and Billy, were well chaperoned at all times. They sat at our household table, the beautiful chandelier Father made for our mother hanging above them, and worked out the logistics. Father would take Abbey and stop and pick up Billy and his mother and then travel on to Aunt Kathleen's. If Auntie were to tire while chaperoning the two, Billy's mother volunteered to keep watch and after the two were safely put to bed, in separate rooms, she would take leave, catch a ride back with Old Man Stovall, the newspaper man, who lives in River John and delivers his newspapers by night. It seemed a good plan, one well thought out. But when dancing occurs the body sometimes fills with animal spirits and the blood stirs.

I fear, because of this incident, my estimate of Billy has soured even further. I now believe him to be a cad as well as foul-mouthed and intemperate. No mother in her right mind would allow her daughter to go with him; not after the Tatamagouche episode with Abbey. Ours is a close community and what is done to one becomes known by all, judged by all and finally censured by all. I swear, everyone in Nova Scotia came to know of their wrong-doing, many a doubtful glance tossed over shoulders whenever passing our family.

The Widow Applegate carefully explained the plans to Abbey. But I could tell the way Abbey shifted her eyes that she cared not a thread about what was said. She impertinently stood, shuffling her foot as the Widow spoke. When the Widow wasn't looking, Abbey even had the audacity to yawn.

"Prove to me you are trustworthy and you will be allowed to attend more socials," the Widow told Abbey. The Widow, on this day, looked somewhat pretty in her lilac print dress. As of late, she took more care regarding her appearance. Clearly she was in love with our father. It showed in how carefully she tended his every need. I no longer brought food to him as he worked in his blacksmith-shop. No, she sometimes even put a small vase with wildflowers on the tray she carried out to him. Also, she hummed as she prepared the tray revealing her affections. Aunt Kathleen took Abbey's hand, held it in hers, and lovingly smoothed the back of Abbey's fingers with her free hand. "She will be good as gold. All Ebenezer's girls are good girls brought up on the word of our Lord. Do not fret. Children are my specialty and mine turned to the good. That be proof enough I am capable of handling things in proper accordance." Auntie sipped her tea and gave Abbey a wink.

But, alas, that wink from Auntie was wasted. It was a wink that said I trust you. And even though Abbey, too, thought the world of our aunt, her blood must have pushed her over the edge of reason.

Oh, Abbey, you are a thoughtless one. I have pondered much over your character, and now my coy sister, you are nearly ruined. And all for kisses far from Auntie's tender eye.

Abbey and Billy were good up to a point. They minded their elders, danced but not too close. Upon their return, Auntie fixed them warm milk sprinkled with cinnamon and saw them off to bed. But bedded they did not remain. Long after our aunt fell into the honey of dreams, the two gathered blankets and set out the door, ever cautious to make no sound. Into the night they went, blinded by passion. They walked to Green Hill and spread out their blankets. After much kissing, or so I am told, they fell into a deep sleep and were awakened by the clanging of the Sunday morning bells.

Aunt Kathleen discovered the errant ones' absence when she went to wake them for morning porridge. How aghast she must have felt, she who promised to keep them safe and has been particularly attentive to us ever since our mother's death, giving us pretties brought back from Halifax. But how could she have known their plans? There was much secrecy in the hearts of those two. Passion can seal the mouth but not the eyes, of that I am certain, as it burns through the veins.

I, too, have felt that burn whenever a certain person, whose name remains unmentioned, nears me. As of late, that knowledge has stirred even though I have tried to ward it off. *Keep your heart closely tethered, Ella.*

Father's anger would not have been so great had he not heard there was a plan afoot to elope, which Abbey, unwisely, let slip, thinking he would go easier on her if marriage was in sight. No child of his, at age fifteen, would disgrace the family in such a way.

The lovers did not even have courtesy enough to return to Aunt Kathleen's that day. They spent the following night in the woods. When Father found Abbey by Willis Creek, dipping her toes in the stream, he grabbed her by the arm and hefted her into the wagon.

He fairly flung her mid-air onto the seat; he later told us this after his temper and vexation cooled.

Billy, upon seeing Father, took off over Green Hill and disappeared into the nearby wooded area, his bare feet fast as elk. Father later said he cared nothing of speaking to him, but he did manage to pick up Billy's shoes from the nearby blanket. He would square things off with Billy at another time and had his shoes as hostage.

So there came the great meeting of Abbey, the Widow Applegate, Billy's parents, our aunt before the Pastor of the first Presbyterian Church. There was much sobbing on Abbey's part. Pastor Smith thought it might be kinder and less strange for Abbey to meet in the Parsonage instead of the church, which seems cold and austere at times. There were also several clergymen present as witnesses to confirm Billy's and Abbey's dalliance.

I do not have a hint of what was said. I only know that Billy and his shoes were suddenly packed off to Halifax, the capital of the Maritime Provinces, where he would live with his father's brother who was an officer in the army.

"Oh, I will surely be sent to hell," Abbey wailed, before the meeting.

"Ruined, I am ruined," she kept repeating.

It was then that I saw another side of the widow. She put her arm around Abbey's shoulder and drew her close. "There, there now," she said. "You are not the first to fall into disgrace. It is not the wrong-doing that catches us up in life. It is how we conduct ourselves afterwards that matters. You will be examined by Doctor Williams in a week's time to ensure there are no serious problems."

At this, Abbey let out a gasp, "Oh, no, I want no one to examine me."

"You have no choice in this matter, young woman. It was decided by your father and me that this is of great importance. We must attend what honor is left you."

Abbey wheeled about in the air, her arms clasped close to her waist. "I will surely die if you make me do this," and she started to cry uncontrollably.

That is when Father spoke up, "No, if anyone is going to die it is Billy," his face grim. It seemed he aged since Abbey's deviousness, dark circles blotted underneath his eyes, his shoulders less squared off in masculine power.

Oh, he would not approve my budding affection for one he knows nothing about. And I vow to keep such thoughts quelled. After all, I have my poetry, my dreams of becoming a doctor, and that might be enough for my life's remainder since I am certain nothing will come of my affections.

Father stood by watching the Widow Applegate and was clearly touched. Tenderness filled his face. But he had been livid earlier over Abbey's escapades. Perhaps what bothered him most was that he felt he lost control and realized his daughters were growing up. He was also ashamed that one of his daughters was now the talk of the town. But the Widow reminded him, "It is through no fault of yours, Ebenezer, that one of your children went astray. Abbey will be enrolled in the Pastor's weekly study on "Walking in the Lord's Way." And she will attend no further socials. I will see to that—not until she is formally betrothed."

Whenever she spoke to Father in this way she held her hands folded as though her words were prayer, and she stepped to and fro in her black button-up shoes with their pointy toes, her dress swaying with each word. Perhaps she held words as dear as I did, but there was no talking poetry with her. For all the good I came to recognize in her, I knew mention of Robert Burns would so enflame her that she would lecture me for hours. She thought him a ruffian, a fickle womanizer.

"He imbibes too much and his hands leap from one woman to another. No poetry, by such a man, is worth the sin it takes to write it. He lusts first after one and then after another. I reckon he will have to answer for his roaming heart come Judgment Day." I said nothing in response. Sometimes one cleaves to silence in order to keep peace and our family was stirred to the hilt by Billy and Abbey.

I made sure, from then on, to hide my book of his work far from her prying eye. No, that book, given to me by mother, took on more meaning, more worth since her death. I thought of her hands when she handed his book of poems to me; hands that stroked my forehead when she lay in bed suffering. That book surely held her hands for all the days to come and the pages themselves were scented with her essence. What I treasured most about receiving Burns' poems was that she nurtured my dream of writing. How often had we taken turns, when no one was around, reading to each other?

No, AFTER THIS FRACAS with Abbey, I will hold, with all my might, my heart's secret. I pledge, nothing will come of my feelings. But how could I know that the terrible searing of fleshly desire would plague me, follow me into even the smallest moment of my waking? I was getting older, a few months past my sixteenth birthday. Many of my friends were now married, building families of their own. I recently attended my closest friend's wedding; Ernestine married Colin after Millie found a new love. Fickle Millie, we call her. She goes through gentlemen as though God himself were keeping score for her.

Father now loaned his best two-passenger surrey, a delicate looking wagon with a sun canopy, to me on a regular basis so that I could travel more easily into town without encumbering him. He spent much time showing me how to harness the horse properly, fasten it snug and how to keep her at a steady gait. You see, my horse, Gabby, was given to me when the MacKay family next door found her not to their liking. She reared whenever one of their children attempted to mount her and Mr. MacKay feared she would hurt his youngest. Her mane was so tangled it was a witch's bridle until I brushed it smooth as silk.

I later heard that the children sometimes taunted Gabby with a prickly thistle against her tender ears, one ear, to this day, still scarred. No wonder the poor thing reared. With me though, she is a good horse, sometimes temperamental but steady on her feet, especially since she took a liking to hearty trots with the surrey. Father bought her from our neighbors for my sixteenth birthday and you cannot imagine my glee.

My friends so envied this opportunity as their fathers would never allow them such favor. But Father said, "You are becoming quite a modern young woman. Trusting you with Gabby will build character. After all, you could be up to worse things," he said, referring to Abbey.

FIVE TOLLS AND A PAUSE

I rode into River John and no sooner stepped down from the surrey, tied my pony to a snortin' post, when a fire alarm sounded
its loud peals from the Church of Scotland in the town's commons.
All able-bodied men ran from hither and yonder, the bells repeated
at intervals. Gabby, angrily tossed her mane and was clearly upset
by the clattering bells. I soothed her haunches with my palm, and
repeated in a soft voice, "There, there now. It is fine. Everything will
be fine." This did not soothe her nerves in the least and I knew only a
hardy trot at a good clip would calm her frayed sensibilities, but she
would have to wait.

Hadley, the baker, rushed out onto his porch, the porch's pillars
as bowed as his legs. He pulled at his suspenders; his thumbs looped
underneath them, belly sticking out as though he hid a watermelon
underneath his shirt, and asked, "Lass, do you know where the fire
be?" His face red as sunset on the Straits.

"I just got here, Mr. Hadley. But there is smoke over the hill to the
east of us. Let me ask some villagers and I will promptly return and
tell you what news is available."

"Sure enough, young lady. I appreciate your thoughtfulness. There
are some shortbreads here when you return—made the way your sisters like, a little walnut pressed to the center of each." He opened the
door and slipped back inside his bake shop, a peal of door bells rang
as he slammed the door shut.

Pastor Smith stuck his head out of the parsonage as I walked the
footpath, little clover sprigs sticking out here and there. His bald

head shone in the light, a long gold chain ran from his pocket, his watch tethered to it. As in many older men, hair snuck down his nose as though ready to escape.

"Good day, Ella. It seems we have a fire at hand."

"Pastor, do you know where it is?" The smoke had finally filtered into town, coloring the air a creamy peach. My throat tickled.

"Judging from the direction, it is out by Widow Millers. Cannot be certain. Do not go quoting me. People have feared for her, being a woman and all, living out there on her own for years. I fancy her husband would turn in his grave if he knew." He cupped his chin in thought. "You cannot tell what might happen by light of day or din of night. Between the French trappers and the Mohawks, Minnie could get herself into a heap of trouble."

"Oh, my God, she is my dear friend," and to escape his blabbering, I bid he give my regards to Mrs. Smith, and quickly ran back to the baker's and fairly broke down his door saying, "It is by Minnie Miller's place." He ran after me, a tied cloth of cookies in his hand. "Do not go forgetting these."

Men clamored in a spirited run, the whole town, or so it appeared, hastened by the fire bells. The MacKenzies still had their white smallpox flag up—even several years after Mr. MacKenzie died. Today it flapped as though quite alive, or perhaps Mr. MacKenzie himself spoke through the wind. His wife declined to remove the last remnants of their life together. Even Minnie's husband's shoes remain near the door as though he might step back into them. Wishful thinking, but perhaps such wishing helps one cope. Do I not, myself, keep a clipping of Mother's hair in my locket? I am a hive of swarming thoughts.

I rushed to the surrey and fairly tumbled into it, gathered the reins and headed to Minnie's place, having no qualms as Father now condoned my visits. He was deeply thankful for the care she had given me when I nearly froze in the woods.

Bells of a horse driven tank of water with a massive reel of hose attached to it clattered over the dirt roadway. Aboard was the bucket brigade and the men were hanging on for dear life, their hats about to scatter alongside the roadway. The mares, known sometimes to be cranky, ran at a good clip. They already looked tired, their tails swishing, ears twitching.

Gabby tossed her head, her black mane streaming in the air. Soot peppered my clothes and my pores clogged with the smoky air which grew thicker the further we went.

No, it cannot be her place. Minnie is diligent regarding upkeep of her house. She is not a casual woman, rather, a hard worker who takes a scythe to her own hay. When recovering from my legtrap wound, she always properly snuffed out the candles. She cautiously refused to put one for reading by my bed because the mattress was made of hay and she said hay easily catches. Surely the fire must be at a neighbor's home, or children who have played with matches in the woods have caused it. The Thomson twins once started a fire that had horse-racing flames that nearly burned down the entire town.

The stench of smoke became stronger the closer we got and a bright haze of fire grew over the horizon—the grasses themselves spitting flames in the air. I cannot begin to tell you the horror of my realization—it was, in fact, Minnie's house. The fire brigade pulled up and the men hooked the hoses. Others started a bucket line and filled pails from Minnie's well, one man dropping the buckets into the well and filling them and handing them off. Flames skirted the roof shingles and a popping sound came from inside.

Several men hosed down the roof. One said, "Douse that roof good. Thin pieces of fuel go first, especially old and dried out shingles." A big burley man, Mr. Witherspoon buttoned his canvas jacket and slipped on his gloves.

"I am going to break down the door. Appears something is jamming it and I do not know what in tarnation it could be," Mr. Witherspoon said. Smoke gushed out from underneath the door casing. The air behind me filled with voices, all giving directions.

"Use caution," I hollered to Mr. Witherspoon. "Look for Minnie inside. Tarry not!"

A fireman, a man I did not know, said to Mr. Witherspoon, "The Lord be with you," and he made a cross sign over his chest. Mr.

Witherspoon tied a cloth over his nose around the back of his head and disappeared, but not before saying, "Now, I am going whole hog."

I yelled, "Minnie, Minnie, if you are in there, come out. Minnie, do you hear me?" A roar so loud it deafened my ears swept through her home, groaned in billowing waves, and a hand yanked me back so fast from where I stood that I felt snatched, utterly snatched.

"Up there on the hill. You go up there, lass, and sit and wait. We will do all we can to save Minnie should she be in there, but the house is going fast. Now off with you," and he shoved me so hard I nearly tripped.

Soon the lead glass windows popped, shattering glass spewed from the windows. How easily things come to an end, I thought. It takes weeks to raise a house, even months, yet fire destroys everything in minutes. Minnie, where are you?

Mr. Witherspoon rushed out, shook his head, "No Minnie. Her flour exploded. The crock was open. She must have been about to make something. Could not get to the attic." He stopped talking, coughed and regained his breath. "No telling her whereabouts. She probably is in town or gone to Halifax." The fire captain handed him a ladle of water. Sweat poured off Mr. Witherspoon's red face, his hat askew. He fairly tore off his outer clothes and cast them aside, panting fast as a hunting dog. "Hot as hell in that place. No amount of grit keeps a man to survive such extremes."

The fire captain ordered his men to keep close surveillance over Minnie's barn and shed, "Make sure no sparks set the rest of her place on fire. There is no saving the house. It will fall, I fear. Watch for grass fires too. Fire spreads fast in dead heat of summer."

Strange, if Minnie was about to bake she would not have gone to town. And she would not have left the lid off her flour larder. No, that is not like her. My legs felt drunken, unable to hold my weight, so I sat as the good man ordered. But sitting made me think more perilous outcomes. I envisioned Minnie's singed bones amongst the rubble; the fire team gathering them once the debris cooled and their dropping her leg-bone, her arm-bone into a flour sack from her shed. They would say things like, "Minnie was a good woman, Christian too. Always gave to the needy. She should not have lived on her own. Dangerous for a woman, especially one well nigh into her seventies."

The house's structural beams were the last to fall and when they did they sprang sparks that twinkled like fireflies. Brigade hands kept dousing the flames and soon only smudges of smoke rose whenever they stirred coals. There was a hissing from water on hot beams and the stones from Minnie's hearth. The hissing reminded me of the rattler we encountered in the privy. How frightened Minnie was that day and how relieved I was to be of assistance. Afterwards, I could conquer anything. But now, witnessing the shambles of my friend's home caused such grief that an overwhelming sense of helplessness filled me.

I thought of those Thomson boys and their deliberate fire for sport, how they were made to scrape blistered paint off the scorched houses and repaint each one. In the middle of summer when humidity is highest, their father stood at the ladder minding his eye on them. But here there was nothing left to scrape or salvage. I had to hold things in. If I cried now there would be no stopping.

When you have loved a place it still stands in the mind as a solid structure. Over and over you enter it, peruse the rooms and sniff the air for familiar scents. Does the air itself gush in where something once stood? Does it make a ghost life of what previously lived? Perhaps that is what is often referred to as a haunting. Was the residue of smoke stirring up strange thoughts in my head?

It was a simple wood house, really. Three rooms in all. Minnie's bedroom, the kitchen- parlor area and a large pantry. The same as what we had at home save an extra bedroom where my two sisters and I slept. The Millers had planned to build another room for a child but none lived. Minnie had but five windows in all and one door. There is much draft with windows, so Father, too, installed few. Also, there was an attic with a dormer window. Minnie said she would never carry a candle into such a place. She hoarded stacks of newspapers, odd trinkets, as well as many storage trunks. It was from these trunks she salvaged clothing for the Micmacs.

Once, I sat beside her on the floor of the attic and she showed me her faded marriage certificate and letters from Mr. Miller. She pressed the marriage certificate to her chest and sighed. Such bright light in her face that day.

The bed Minnie had made for me when recovering from my legtrap wound, a funny shipping box, was turned into a settee after Father took me home and she had thrown a colorful quilt over it. How many times had we sat upon it as we took our tea? And what of her turnips, the beets, strange things collected on her window sills? What of her butter churn, her mementoes from her husband? No, a world without my friend loomed large and hugely empty, and a Minnie without her own home would be utterly devastated.

The fire brigade hosed her shed and barn. "Make certain there is not a single spark left alive," the fire captain instructed. "How are you, young lady? Holding up, I presume?"

"I am doing fine, but there is much to be concerned about. It is not like Minnie to have cooking things out and to suddenly disappear. I fear she has come to harm."

"Do not go fretting. Women sometimes trot off for necessary ingredients. Anyhow, that is my best guess. Better head home lest your father stew over your whereabouts. I will have Mr. Witherspoon apprise you of any news."

Brushing insects off my clothes, I stood and thanked him. The sight of her missing house, deformity of structure, was overwhelming. No more to be done here; the house cremated as though it were a living body. Little drifts of smoke rose—the charred remains setting off steam. Worry never fails to host an anvil and its weight is nothing but cumbersome. So, I boarded the surrey with the most listless intent. Gabby neighed, and we headed back to town. The early evening was lackluster, not even the setting sun lifted my spirits. I looked back at my friend's place, a lump fat as a stone lodged in my throat. Tears pushed at the backs of my eyes. There was no need to hurry. I tugged the reins and pleaded Gabby slow herself.

Perhaps a stop at Meadow Brook would soothe me, especially if I dipped my feet in the water. I would indeed gather composure there. *Where, oh where are you Minnie?*

From Out of the Woods When Suddenly

I looped Gabby to a willow and sat on the moss covered ground, my feet soaking in the stream. Ragweed grew in profusion along the hillside; Father calls it Stinking Willie which is what the weed is called in Scotland. Thistles too, and skunk cabbage lined the brook. Every so often a trout fell back into the water with a heavy splash. Hulls of leaves and twigs boated their way downhill on the smooth current. I imagined fairies and elves hidden in their storage compartments, the wisest fairy offering travel directions. Minnie, whom I failed to put from my mind, became the fairest of fairies in this imaginary parade, bright yellow wings, and shoes of the brightest silver with red ribbon ties. Her hair was no longer gray; rather she wore plaited braids pinned into a crown atop her head accentuating her delicate features.

The slow lap of water wound its way downstream—a ribbon of serenity. For hours, I could sit listening to it. No matter what falls in, no matter who wades through, the brook sticks to its course. Water is a good student to the ways of life. It swells and empties itself without a care. *Ella, spill your head of cares. Let the fire you just witnessed float downstream and out to the ocean.* Those words kept harking at me, but one must bide time with sorrow just as I did when Mother died. But, still, I could not cease my obsession with my friend, the stories we shared.

Minnie and her husband spent many months when they built their house and cleared their land. Husband and wife, side by side. They also thinned wooded thickets so they could see over the hills onto three neighboring farms. They had a cold spring house and in the hot summers they stored milk, cream and eggs and occasionally meat there. Minnie said they sometimes dipped themselves with cold water from the spring, each taking turns as they ladled water over the other. Well, all was gone now except the outhouse, shed and barn, plus the spring house.

Mosquitoes hummed their delight over Gabby's and my presence and I swatted the ones on my arms—huge welts rising. My feet were cold from the water so I dried them off with the hem of my dress, my toes a bluish white. Weary of smoke and things that tear at the heart, I stretched out on the moss, and gazed at the sky, a few wisps of long thin clouds above. Had Minnie returned to her place by now? Such sadness she would feel upon seeing her loss.

No sooner had I lain down when Gabby suddenly whinnied, and grew restless, pawing the ground. She tugged heartily at her tether and tossed her mane, her eyes nearly ablaze. Behind me, the clack of moving bushes, a thrashing. I sat straight up. My heart raced. Could it be the Mohawks?

Instead, as if ordained by some heavenly body, Stands Like a Tree appeared.

"What are you doing here, Ella?"

My face turned crimson. His chest was bare. The only other man I ever saw shirtless was my father as he stood shaving at the water basin in the kitchen. Stand Like a Tree's legs, right down to his moccasins, were covered in leggings of dark hair. Avert your eyes, Ella, I told myself, as though the man were totally bare. Yet I stood staring at his bronze chest with the little deer skin medicine bag that hung from his neck. For the life of me I could not come to my senses.

"Did you hear what happened to Minnie's place?" I asked him, hoping conversation would clear my head, make me feel less a nerve-hopping-jumble.

"Yes, I was just there. Her place is a sorry sight. Do you know her whereabouts?"

"Nobody seems to know where she is. I thought you might know. Do you suppose she met with a terrible fate?" I paused, regained by bearings. "French trappers have caused endless trouble these days. They might have harmed her." No sooner had those words spilled from my lips than I wished they remained stuck far back in my mouth. I attempted to seal my lips with the back of my hand. "I will call some Micmac braves together and we will search. The fire captain was still at her place combing through the coals when I stopped by. He does not think Minnie was burned to death."

"Please," I urged. "Do not think me impulsive or insistent but news came my way that there is a marauding band of trappers who are known to imbibe in much whiskey. They are worth consideration. Our neighbors say they are a fire-water totting bunch." Stands Like a Tree gave me a curious look but said nothing. He shuffled his feet and swayed a bit to one side. Clearly, he was holding something back. And when he spoke, I was much aggrieved.

"My father, Lone Cloud, died. We buried him just before the Sun Dance. It was not expected so soon. I am weary with sorrow. Sorrow for my father and sorrow for Minnie. I will look into Minnie's disappearance but only after I regain my strength. A man weakened by sorrow does no good when sent on a mission. I must first sleep and I must eat."

With his mention of death, I broke down sobbing. I sobbed for my mother, for my father who sometimes picked up something she had made, and held it tight to his heart. Never, of course, in front of the Widow Applegate. I sobbed for myself, for my ineptitude at keeping Minnie safe. And, finally, I cried for Minnie and for Stands Like a Tree. It seemed the entire world, at the moment, was smoky with sorrow.

Stands Like a Tree moved slowly toward me and took my hand in his. "Do not go fearing, Ella, for what you do not know. There is plenty to fear in a lifetime. Spare yourself."

The way he said Ella conjured my mother's words, "My Bella Ella." It seemed as though she now spoke through him. I pondered the miracle of this. Or was this just a case of being a smitten girl? He smelled of sage and his words rose from so deep a place inside his chest they sounded like drums. I desired nothing more than laying my head against him. But that I should not do, and did not do. Instead, I breathed him in so fully that he would travel home inside me.

"You best be on your way. Your pony is restless and the sky is closing, nightfall soon on the rise. I will keep you apprised of Minnie; even the slightest word will find its way to you."

He let go of my hand and walked up alongside the stream, his shoulders so wide I thought they must have once carried the entire Micmac settlement's belongings. Sure footed, and graceful in his movement, he thinned into the distance. The air itself seemed to lose a beat as he finally disappeared behind a weave of willows. But I was most assured that if anyone could find Minnie it would be Stands Like a Tree.

Stands Like a Tree
at Meadow Brook

I could feel the young girl they call Ella, her blue eyes like small birds resting on my shoulders as I took my departure. No, I would not look back, encourage her. My people teach young men to cleave to the old ways. Do not solicit attention from the settlers' females. Do not cross the line that carries spirits of your past. On the other hand, the colonists themselves have been known to take a Micmac woman as wife. Once wed to a white person, such women give up their original ways and no longer wear their coarse blue clothing or their traditional pointed hats. They are ordered to give up their beadwork and shells which they trade as currency; even their basket-making is discouraged. Wampum gives Micmac women independence. But, shut off from their traditions these women suffer greatly. Many stories are told of their loneliness, how a Micmac woman can pine to death for the sisterhood of her people.

One woman, in particular, her isolation so great, refused to eat and in childbirth both infant and mother died. The baby weighed but a thread and was shriveled as an old man. Those who saw him called him *Sorrow's Child*. This story is repeated to our young women to discourage them from taking up with a colonist. Luckily, an old midwife, half Micmac herself, buried the mother and baby according to our ways. She secretly dressed the mother in a hide tunic and long skirt. Once the pine box was closed no one knew, except our people who later showered kindness upon the midwife.

And, even I, as a youngster in the household of the pious ones, was not allowed my original clothes. No, they dressed me like one of theirs—clothes telling me I was other than myself. To spite them I tore at my clothes making holes. The pious one's wife would say, "What a little ruffian, always getting his clothes torn apart." And she would ask, "Who did you fight with today?"

Under such questioning there is no recourse but to remain silent, my eyes dead to the sight of her. "One more time young man and you will get a thrashing. See then if you go tearing your breeches up in fist fights. When Mr. O'Brien returns, he will take you to the shed and tan your bottom good."

FOR SOME TIME, I STOOD, hidden behind willows, on the trace to Meadow Brook, watching young Ella. A year back, on the ice, I found much favor in her voice and saw spirits rise from her words. Now, as a young woman, her hair has become the color of chestnuts, skin without blemish. By far, Ella is the prettiest thing upon the land, and humble too. Minnie spoke of her with high regard. Minnie herself must have seen the sparks flare in my eyes whenever I looked at Ella. She must have known my thoughts as we rested the child on her bed when I found her nearly frozen in the woods.

But, I am a man bound to my people so I steel myself against contrary thoughts that divide me. A divided man does no good for his people. Opposing thoughts will eventually slay a person. Our medicine men have chants for such a man with split nature. I had just returned from my father's burial and from the Sun Dance where I assisted the sick, myself four days without water, and so traveled to the brook to rid my thirst and cleanse my body. But first, horror of horrors, there was Minnie's place in ashen shambles. The fire captain believed she was out on errands, that there was no need to fear otherwise. That came as relief. Through Minnie's friendship and kindness a page turned in my opinion of the settlers.

A charitable heart becomes known throughout the land and is much valued. So, as time passed, many Micmac families began to watch over her. We bring her moose and partridge, of which she is particularly fond. She also likes ruffed grouse. She is called Good

Woman Minnie by our people. She is known to love this child, Ella, and fastens her attention towards helping her too.

With great fierceness, I attempt to ward off thoughts of the young girl, but dreams of Ella sometimes arise and race through my body. Little can be done about dreams, their apparent wilderness. They become as wild horses. Feverish is my sleep when dreams of her arise. If awakened, I splash cold water on my face and chest to quell the fire. Before sleep, I ask Glooscap to watch over my dreams, but sometimes he is attending others in far greater need. Glooscap's power can move hills and rivers and he can change people into animals. One such Micmac, a man of bad nature, was turned into a rat. This came as warning to my people to walk in the ways of honor. On such nights of the body's storm, I also ask my father, Lone Cloud, to keep me taut with courage and to bless my journey amongst our people. Who pines more than a son who has lost his father before truly knowing him? A lesson from him stays with me on such nights of torment. *Take a thistle to bed and lay it across your chest. Barbs from it will wake you as you thrash from dreams.*

No, Ella must never gain awareness of my feelings.

Also, she does not know what I found at Minnie's, the head-roach. No, she would set off on her own to gain retribution. But what I have discovered tells of Minnie's fate and there is no time to lose if there is any hope for her safety. After a short rest, Stands Like a Tree must lose no ground.

Here We Go Again

"Father, do you know where Minnie is or where those bedeviled trappers might be?"

Candlelight splashed across the supper table. The Widow Applegate quietly chewed her bread and relief spread throughout me that she seemed not in a talkative mood. Sprigs of curls stuck out from her top knot and with all that hair pulled away from her face her nose seemed sharper and longer. My sisters, thank goodness, were at Aunt Kathleen's helping out since Auntie had a severe case of dyspepsia.

It was comforting to know that I would have the bed entirely to myself. There was much to contemplate before sleep closed my eyes. "There is some talk in town that they were seen on Fitzpatrick Mountain. Why in tarnation do you ask, Ella?"

The Widow Applegate shot me a piercing, see-straight-through-you glance. She tapped her spoon against the tabletop waiting for my reply, her face dour. This made me think it wise that the original word-maker coupled sour with dour. The Widow often seemed both.

"Father, you know the man who once worked here on the fence posts and found me nearly frozen, carried me to Minnie's? He is about to search for her and he will need some inkling as to her whereabouts. I think the fur trappers are responsible."

"What makes you think the trappers have anything to do with her disappearance?"

I looked down at my bowl of buttermilk soup with its chunks of potatoes and corn nuggets. *What, oh, what to say? Did Stands Like a*

Tree not concur it might be them? But I cannot tell Father this. Did I misinterpret Stands Like a Tree? I mentioned the trappers to him and it seemed he agreed they were sometimes up to no good, therefore suspect. Yes, I believe he does think it them. My thoughts become so jumbled in Stands Like a Tree's presence that I feel a bit like a humming bird who expends energy at a rapid rate. "Father, both of us have heard stories of their ways—some notorious, such as stealing from farmers' wives the milk they have drawn. One French trapper even stole Mrs. Frazier's cow straight from the pasture and the mischievous man was later found wandering through the woods with the cow on a lead. What a funny sight that must have been. Cows belong in pastures not in forests." I chuckled over the thought.

"Eat some soup, Ella, before it chills," the Widow said. I gave her a cursory look, took a few spoonfuls of the buttery soup.

"You, yourself, told me that Father. And our neighbors, the MacKays, spoke of the trappers bilking the Hudson Bay Company of sea otter furs they hid at Olson's fort." I eyed the Widow for a moment to register her mood and quickly cast my glance back to the table. "And we must not forget, Father, that it was one of their poorly maintained traps that snapped shut on my ankle."

Father's face grew serious. "Just because Minnie is missing does not mean that the trappers took her. You are jumping to conclusions, Ella. Her situation may very well be quite innocent—off to visit relatives in Pictou or Halifax. You fret too much." He sneezed, drew his handkerchief from his pocket and blew his nose. "Albeit a sad loss, her house and all, still, they found no Minnie Miller in the charred remains. Keep that in mind, young woman."

Needless to say, I shifted in my seat under the stern instruction of his words. My eyes felt heavy and the room grew dim. Still, one cannot easily shake worry, especially when one knows with certainty that life does not always go according to one's preconceptions.

"And do not go trotting off in search of her," added the Widow Applegate. "I heard of your escapades before your mother died. Poor woman, to worry so on your account as she lay dying. Mischief, that is what you were up to."

"That is quite enough, Elizabeth. Never repeat what you just said to my daughter." Father's face grew flushed, his mouth narrow and drawn, he pushed his soup bowl away and gruffly said, "There is always more to things than first appear. Ella is an unusually smart and sensitive young woman."

The Widow quickly cleared her bowl as well as Father's, and without a word she retired to the bedroom, shutting the door softly behind her. Muffled sobs could be heard and I felt sorry she was reprimanded in such a way in front of me. Her humiliation was difficult to absorb on a day of so many events. I wished for nothing more than closure and for the moon to rise and wash us all in its benevolent light.

OF THORNS AND GOODBYES

Into the forest I hurry. My Micmac ancestors with me. Wind at my back.

First, I must secure the rock for seasoning my blade, sharpen my knife, and then search the northern woods where the Mohawks were last seen. They hunt partridge this time of year, half of them by the shorelines to catch fish, the other half in search of birds. Surefooted, I walk soft as a cougar in search of prey.

But I hold no real intentions of using my knife, not anymore. The more we fight amongst ourselves the more we diminish our numbers; all of us are the original peoples on this part of the earth. Why hurt each other?

I, Stands Like a Tree, recently took an oath: *I will spread no blood on the floor of the earth. The leaves and moss are saturated with it. I will search for my friend, Minnie, with exactitude and peace. There is already too much blood spilled from disagreement and greed. I will break the spilled-blood-chain even though I carry a knife. It is the power I endow upon the blade that will keep me safe. It is my protector. I will sew my lips with a needle-bone. Spread bloodroot's sap across my face. Season the knife's blade with Grandfather's chants, with the blessings of the sacred bear, and with the rock best known for sharpening knives. Thank the rock for its firmness, for how it saves my life again and again.*

TODAY, IN SADNESS, I, Stands Like a Tree, recall the ceremonial dog that was killed by my people as a sacrifice to their grief over my father's death, how the dog howled as the knife pierced its chest. In that moment something changed inside me. I felt myself awash with the cries of others, their laments pouring through me.

Regarding my father, I recall that he died quickly after injury from a thorn that pierced through his moccasin. Regrettably, he took little notice. But within a few days his foot became inflamed and the poisons traveled his leg and eventually stopped his heart. It was so sudden, this rise of poison, that no medicine man was capable of helping him.

Before his passing, my father was reclined in his birch bark death-bed; his funeral held before his passage. This, the custom of the Micmac people. And though saddened, I was pleased my father did not linger in agony. Since he did not linger, he was not left behind as my people traveled to the shores for oysters which are abundant at this time of year. I was most grateful his closing eyes held sight of his people during that last breath.

Father quietly spoke his last words as he asked the gathered Micmacs to remain loyal to their traditions, traditions that were rapidly being destroyed by the Christian settlers. He went on to say that the thorn given to him by Glooscap was a gift that rendered his safe passage to the stars. The Grand Council of Micmacs nodded in agreement; Yes, the thorn, indeed, was a gift to Lone Cloud, a man they revered for his honesty and perseverance.

To me, who stood by his death bed, he said, " My firstborn, Stands Like a Tree, you will feel my presence as you travel underneath a lone cloud that sails the sky to mark the day of my death. Look for this cloud after the passage of twelve moons. Take guidance from the sky which never fails to speak its wisdom." Then his face became as a mask. His chest no longer rose with the tides of breath, and peace smoothed his well creased face. I deeply mourned my lost days with him.

It was at that moment that anger rose inside me; anger for the white people who took me from him when I was but a child. Those first few nights in the strangers' home, I cried myself to sleep. They foolish-ly thought that the much cherished tea laced with honey, something settlers seemed to love, would quell my loneliness, but instead, it only swelled until it crowded the small back room assigned me.

The settlers thought they had done right by my father when they brought me to the home of this pious clergyman in River John when I was but five. Their family saved a Micmac from starvation and from heathenish ways—words I overheard when the settler family thought me asleep.

That is what they believed. But it was their God of righteousness they aimed to please after stripping my people of what was rightfully Micmac land—our great territory shrank to nothing as the seasons passed. *Let us live amongst you* became, *Let us force you further back into the wilderness.* As I grew older, I witnessed firsthand how the colonists broke promise after promise.

At first, the government offered assistance in the form of blankets, grain, oats and flour. Then those in charge of distribution started to quibble amongst themselves on account of how much we peoples cost and no further help arrived. Rumor claimed the colonists kept the supplies for themselves. Even a single blanket was shared by an entire Micmac family, those on the ends of the pine sleeping mats tugging for warmth. As animals became scarce so did their hides which were used for warmth and for clothes.

Several of the colonists claimed we were Porcupine Indians due to the quillwork our women sold in town, but I am proud to call myself Micmac. Stands Like a Tree is not any Porcupine Indian, although my anger can sometimes be sharp as a porcupine's quill.

WHAT WOULD I TELL ELLA, should opportunity arise, of my heritage? Would I say there is more to seasoning the blade than sharpening it across a power stone? Would I say one must season the heart too?

No, I must not carry her into my thoughts. She is, after all, of those peoples who hurt my family and many others through starvation and disease. But then, what of Minnie? And with this thought of Minnie, Stands Like a Tree's wandering thoughts cease.

Inside the Heart of a Tree

M y heart beat hard against my ribs. A drumming sound that traveled all the way up into my ears. In such drumming were my people. This rendered comfort to know that visions of my people traveled with me. When your people travel with you, your strength is increased. My shoulders grew broader. Power was within me.

Ahead stood the large oak that stored my sharpening stone and I sighed with relief it was not further into the woods. This tree I named Grandfather Oak for its width and stature. It is a magnificent tree, one that does not stoop, rather, stands firm against the winds. Working my hand inside the burl storage place on the tree's trunk, I was suddenly taken aback by a nesting bird that flew out and angrily beat its wings at me. Had she thought my sharpening stone an egg? Laughter rose from deep inside me.

It was a day splashed with golden sunlight, a fine day for searching out the Mohawks.

With the stone in one hand and my knife in another, I ran the blade along its surface carefully back and forth, working off little peels, and then wiped the blade down on my leather strop. The waterstone was cool in my hand, its surface flat, and every so often I dipped it in a nearby puddle left from the last rains. A waterstone must be made wet every so often in order to render the best results. I worked seated cross-legged, the stone held upon my leg with one hand, the other working the blade.

Be firm, the knife seemed to say as I quietly drew it along the stone's surface. Perhaps my entire life was reflected in this blade worked against stone. The waterstone was my father, and I the knife's blade. The stone spoke of patience and the blade reflected my future, how it must be cut with a fine line.

As I rubbed my knife against stone there rose within me veneration for all the earth bestows and I felt naked and empty. This meant that the knife, too, was momentarily naked and empty. Birds chattered in treetops and the sweet scent of leaves rinsed through my hair. For the first time, the oneness of all life entered my flesh—I was the stump upon which I sat, the sky and all the animals of the forest. Onto the steel blade, reverence spilled from my lips. "Blade, you are my soul. My soul shines like the sun."

This somewhat surprised me because soul talk was Christian talk and I thought myself emptied of all such teachings. It now seemed my own Micmac background and the teachings of the people I lived with in River John comingled. A few years back I would have been aghast at such a coupling of beliefs.

The heart of the tree protected my waterstone while the heart of my body drove common sense through my veins. Was I wiser now? This could not be known since no man truly knows himself. But I do know that the burl of the tree, or outside heart as grandfather called it, is made though stress and that this kind of hardwood is much sought after—turned into fire-stove mantels and furniture because of its endurance. I, too, want to endure. Not only endure, but thrive. I want, also, to leave stories for the future—stories that tell of my way on earth so that one day, should luck provide a son, I will fortify that child with the knowledge I gathered as I canoed and walked upon the earth.

CAREFULLY, I TUCK THE WATERSTONE back into the oak's burl, thankful to be finished, and I splash water onto my face from a nearby stream. The water tastes good as it falls into my mouth and I drink heartily. The water is cool so I splash some upon my chest and brow. In the water there are the spirits of all the fish that swim here and the plants that sink their roots down into the soil. Rocks, too, speak their sacred words as water gushes over them, everything imbued with sacred presence.

Again, I set out. With fever, I search for broken twigs that tell of the Mohawks passage, my eyes also attentive for any signs of broken ground. From my earliest time of memory, I recall my father saying that every Micmac feared the Mohawks. Each morning he would pray to the sun asking for protection of his family. And, for the most part, his prayers worked and we were left alone.

Many a family aligned themselves to the French and it was with their arrival that Christianity reached our shores, Catholicism in particular. But I have fought for independence and cling to the old ways. Micmacs, in general, get along best with the French because there are not so many compared to the English and Scottish. Since they are fewer in numbers less Micmac land is confiscated. The French are mostly interested in trapping for furs and return to France once they have made a good sum of money.

ONWARD

Suddenly, there falls the rustling of feet and the birds grow still. Dust rises. From the dust, I conclude there must be five grown men on the trail. Although there are now no birds to be seen, still I hear bird calls and know others have spotted me and that they have split up and are sending signals to one another. I dart behind a pine. There is anger in their footfalls. I reach down and touch the head of my knife, asking it protect me. My breath grows still as nighttime and my eyes water from intense seeing. Ahead, the leaves shake and the Mohawks break into sight, their vivid head wear bloodred.

From behind me, snapping twigs tell me one or two are about to sneak up on me. Just as I turn, the larger of the two men says, "Why, it is Stands Like a Tree."

He tells me his name is White Owl and that he has no quarrel with me. He pants out of breath. His face is streaked in dust and he smells of hemlock.

I release my hand from the knife's protection and ask, "How is it that you know my name?"

"We have been watching you for years. Your father was Lone Cloud, a man we feared, so we took notice of each member of his family throughout many years, even the white ones in River John where you grew up."

This tracking of me, as though I were a hunted animal, angers me, yet I reveal nothing in my face. "Why are you traveling Micmac Land?"

White Owl scowls and clearly I have breached the confines of his patience. His face flames in anger yet his muscles reveal restraint as they tighten. His fists remain taut. The others gather in closer to him as though he were in need of their protection. There are, as earlier suspected, five in all. They are much shorter than White Owl but just as fierce. One of them holds a war club which he swings as though to taunt me.

"We travel your land in search of a French trapper. Last winter he stole from us a valuable white sable which one of our people shot." He stops talking and swats a mosquito on his cheek. "He escaped from our wrath and we have been told he hides an old woman up near Brown's old fort. This trapper goes by the name of Louie DeVaile. Have you heard of him?"

Little pools of light glint off White Owl's nose, his brow furrowed. I fear he will not believe my answer. "No, I never heard that name."

"Have you searched Brown's fort?" No sooner do I ask when it hits me that White Owl spoke of someone being hidden.

"Do you know who he hides?" I shift my weight from one foot to the other.

"Your friend the Minnie woman. We heard he dropped a head-dress roach belonging to us at her burned out home. It was a trick to make you and everyone else believe we took her."

White Owl becomes even more serious, his face set. His chest is huge and he must be a formidable opponent. His name is said with great fear by those who tell of his ways, always a fierce warrior. One who shows no mercy, no matter the cries from his opponent.

"The French man knows we are after him. To throw us off track he creates a diversion and knows you will be on the hunt for us." He backs away from me and so do the others. They follow with their eyes his every move.

"Why have you taken so long to retaliate?" I ask.

White Owl shakes his head. "This is not retaliation. This is justice. He eluded us but we did not forget that the man stole our brother's sable. We had other, more important, scores to settle first." He yawns, covers his mouth with the back of his hand.

"We leave Stands Like a Tree alone. We have no quarrel with him today."

"Wait. Please wait." White Owl turns back to face me. The woods become noisy with bird calls and this time they are the real birds.

"What do you want?"

"Do not harm Minnie. She has nothing to do with your quarrel. Promise me no harm will come to her."

"And what, Stands Like a Tree, will you do in return for such favor?"

There was nothing comparable to offer. We Micmacs are no match for him, our numbers greatly dwindled. We are not even powerful enough now to offer him safety. What can I offer but empty promises? There are goods though. Could I offer him blankets? What about maple syrup? Or even an exchange of hunting grounds? For that I would have to barter with the council, and we have so few supplies.

"Let me ponder. I would want to honor White Owl with something worthy of his good nature. Let me speak to my people."

"Yes, you talk. I promise the white woman's survival but we will not lead her from the forest. She will have to find her own way back. And a warning. Do not follow us. You best heed my words if Stands Like a Tree plans to reach old age."

With that, he left. The woods swallowed him and soon it was as though we had not met. Hopefully, White Owl would keep his word. Still, worry grew heavy inside me. Would Minnie be safe? What if she tried to protect the French man? It is hard to predict what a woman like Minnie might do in the heat of a crisis. Most certainly the thief will meet with trouble.

I knew little of the French colony, but I did know they trafficked in liquor to rob the Mohawks of reason when it came time to trade. For a man to steal what belonged to another was wrong. It would be made right. Of that, there was certainty. I also heard a French man who visited the pious one's home where I had been taken as a child, describe us Micmac people as the clay-red race, light-footed and having neither letters nor laws nor settled habitations. Other than those things, my knowledge of them was limited.

Ella, I must tell Ella. She was right. It was not the Mohawks. But first I must go back to the tree where my sharpening stone lay inside the burl. I must ask something of the oak. It must speak to the Blade of my Being and tell me whether it is wise to follow the Mohawks.

ELLA PRESSES HER EAR TO THE WINDOW

Did I hear the crying of an animal? It was dark outside and I could not be certain. Was an animal in pain? I put down the candle and walked to the window. There was an ocean of darkness in the yard. Not even the stars were out and the full moon had passed for the month. Everyone was sleeping. My sisters had returned from Aunt Kathleen's and were in bed. Because they were back extra caution was needed.

I pressed my ear tight to the window. No, it was not an animal. It was the hoot of an owl. This troubled me because I recently read that an owl was a symbol of death, a foreshadowing of what was to come. Had I read this in the Bible or was it in a book on mythology that I buried in a box in Father's shop for fear the Widow Applegate would find it and say, "Ella is now studying witchcraft like those heathens in New England?" Yet, the repeated hoots were dissimilar from an owl. Could it be a message? Both Stands Like a Tree and Minnie knew birdcalls. Perhaps one of them was attempting to gain my attention.

Stealthily, I headed to the door, a candle in one hand. I must not awaken anyone. Perhaps I could get to the barn with just the candle and once inside use it to start the lantern to cast a larger circle of light. Ever so carefully I opened the heavy wood door. The air was moist with dew and scent from golden heather floated in the air. The candle flickered in a frightful way and I worried it would soon go out, so I cupped the flame with my free hand to make a shield. My nightdress's hem swept against the wet grasses making a swish-like sound that reminded me of the rattlesnake I escorted out of Minnie's privy.

The barn door squeaked and I hoped not to stir Lucinda into a loud moo. She had been moved inside due to a weepy abscess. The barn smelled of manure, hay and things both alive and dead—a rich pungent odor. With caution I placed the candle on a barrel and lifted the lantern off its nail-hook. The hoots could be heard more clearly now and I worried this would disturb my sleeping family. Ever so carefully, I removed the glass frame from the lantern and turned up the wick. Luckily, the candle's flame took and the lantern cast a warm glow.

Lucinda's plaintive eyes studied me and I went to her and patted her forehead. Her eyes were runny from the abscess, but Lucinda was expected to pull through just fine. She was still young and would have many more seasons in the pasture. I picked up a cloth and tenderly wiped her eyes. The cow nestled her wet black nose into my shoulder.

Erratic hoots continued and were closer now than before. They seemed not far from the barn. I scurried across the dew-wet grasses to the side of the barn where Father stored the surrey, a lean-to roof protecting it from bad weather, and held the lantern high in the air. What if it was not Minnie or Stands Like a Tree? What if it was a ploy to get me outside while mischief took place inside where my unsuspecting family slept?

Darkness made the world a more dangerous place. The world was without limit in the dark and the dark could certainly swallow one up. Should I have ventured out on my own? Shadows flickered in the lantern light, making them sinister and filled with mystery. I wanted to return to the comfort of my bed, the predictability of comfort itself. I thought I heard the flap of wings. Instead, it was the slap of nearby bushes. Yes, something rustled out there in the dark. It must be an animal, I tried to convince myself to keep fear at bay. Fear always has a way of clouding judgment. *Oh, keep me safe. I ought never to have questioned the Lord.*

"Who is there?" I asked and only silence answered. A silence so loud it rang in my ears. The lantern's flame roared and I began to know fear like I had never known it before.

A Hole in the Darkness

"Over here, Ella, it is me." The voice emanated from behind the wild rose bushes and the words tumbled like rushing rain on a roof top.

"Who are you?" But it seemed I knew. A sigh of relief filled me, the night now less large. I was not alone out here in the endless world that cranked my imagination up to unimaginable proportions.

"It is I, Stands Like a Tree," came a whisper. "I cannot be seen. I am being followed—they are at some distance—and I must exert extra caution." He sounded tired. "Turn down your lantern. You can see me squatted nearby when I strike a sulfur stick."

There in the stick's glow was a golden face awash in shadow and light. He picked up a twig and lit it and cast the burnt-out sulfur stick aside. "Over closer," he said as he pushed his hair back from his shoulder. He smelled of pine, hemlock and sweat. All those scents I remembered from when I was carried from the woods to Minnie's house. "Sit down," he instructed. "Both of us will become a shield against the light if we turn sideways."

"Why are you being followed?" I fumbled with the buttons on my nightdress to make sure they were indeed buttoned. I thought myself foolish clothed in such a way in front of a man.

"I went against my word to the Mohawks for fear of Minnie's safety. I was told not to follow and follow is exactly what I did. The tree with the burl where I keep my stone told me to guide her to safety. I could not turn away from such a friend as Minnie. I was asked to give the Mohawks something in return, but there was no time. Things happened so fast."

"Then she is alive!" Tingles of excitement shot through me. Now the night was no longer frightful and I delighted that my friend Minnie amongst the living.

"Yes, she is alive, but is badly scraped up by tree branches and bushes from her flight away from Brown's old fort, plus she broke her arm. Minnie is now staying with a band of my people. Louie, the French fur trapper, burnt her house down and left a head roach on the ground to make everyone believe the Mohawks had taken her."

"Why did he do that?"

"The Mohawks had a dispute they needed to settle with him. He was a very bad man. Ruthless in how he conducted business. He thought the villagers in River John would be in pursuit of the Mohawks in order to find Minnie, and he would escape their wrath." Stands Like a Tree shook his head in amazement. "If White Owl, the Mohawk chief, and his band of Mohawks were killed then no one would know he stole what rightfully belonged to them—a pure white sable which fetches a hefty sum."

Stands Like a Tree shifted his weight before continuing. "He was not able to sell the sable until he got rid of those who it rightfully belonged to. The Hudson Bay Company wants no trouble from any of us and refuses to buy furs that cannot be verified."

Stands Like a Tree snuffed out the twig's flame. "Ella, I must ask a favor. I need you to go to our inland settlement up near Split Lightning Tree and ask that a canoe be provided me. It must be hidden near the lobster crates and rock pilings on Kajeboogwek's shore. It must be well covered in willows. I must make myself invisible until their anger blows over."

"But I do not know the shore you speak of." I hoped my ignorance seemed not distasteful and I took a deep breath. His name of places so different from my own. The ground was cold on my bare feet and the air silent, a silence that rings with a high pitch making one think trouble is afoot.

"You know where it is. It is John's Bay. I gave you our Micmac name which means *flowing through a solitary place* in the event someone else refers to it by that name. Besides, you yourself will not be taking the canoe there. My people will carry it and stow it away."

Irritation filled me regarding the words, *My People*. Was I not a human like him? Surely I am as much his people as anyone. But I told myself not to stew.

"All I need is for you to let my people know the canoe must be provided quickly—quick as a whistle that breezes through the forest."

Why is it that my words or ignorance make me seem child-like? But now was not the time to wrestle with my imperfections. Perhaps I could also visit with Minnie and see if she is all right.

"Yes, I will do it first thing tomorrow. But I am worried for your safety. Please take no chances and stay well hidden."

I stood up from my squatted position as did the Micmac. Stands Like a Tree was close. I could feel his moist breath upon my cheek. It seemed the fluttering of a small bird, an extraordinarily beautiful bird with feathers of every color and a song, so beautiful, was housed in its throat. One would most certainly die listening to it. Something grew restless inside me. What is this strange feeling my heart speaks of? I am pulled towards this Micmac man. I wish nothing more than to rest my head upon his chest and feel his skin fasten to mine.

Oh, lovely golden skin that sings of the sun, which rings of the ocean's waves, that smells of the forest and of deep, deep mystery. I am a girl at the very doorstep of becoming a young woman. And here, the one I now pine for almost daily, and warn myself never to speak his name out loud, stands beside me.

What would Father say? What admonishments would be in store from the Widow who now carries the weight of our household? If they thought Abbey headed towards trouble, most certainly they would think me more wanton and bound straight for the devil's door.

Into his hand, Stands Like a Tree took mine. He squeezed it. "Do this for me, Ella." It was both a question and request. I, of course said yes. There was much more I wanted to say, although the utmost decorum was required.

Yet, my hesitancy was not too great because I asked him, "What is that scent that flowers the air?" It was all pervasive.

"It is sweet grass for purification."

He lifted my face to his, his breath like candied mint, and all he said was, "Ella, Ella," those words never more sacredly spoken. He burrowed his nose in my hair, inhaled deeply and then like the night when I first saw him on the ice, he pushed me aside and disappeared into the woods.

For hours, or so it seemed, I stood where he left and could not convince myself to return to bed. I stood where his feet had stood, hoping I might absorb him. A mighty hole remained in the darkness. I looked to the sky, but still no light shone. With great reluctance I headed back to the house. Ever-so-quietly I lifted the latch and let myself in.

Someone was Awake

"Tell me, tell me Ella, who you saw last night?" Abbey asked as she spooned her porridge, her eyebrow arched to an inquisitive twist; hair bushed in disarray from sleep and her white muslin nightdress crumpled as a discarded note.

"None of your business. Do you not have enough to worry with your upcoming marriage to Billy?"

Really, my primary thought was to get the surrey ready to race into town and make my way to Split Lightning Tree, seeing Minnie foremost in my mind. I also needed to relay Stands Like a Tree's request. But there was no doubt that appeasement to Abbey's inquisitive nature was important. She would tell if I ignored her.

"I watched you slip into the barn and again when you came out with Father's lantern. You remained to the side of the barn for some time. Furthermore, there was a figure by the rose patch and then you turned down the lantern." She had a curl to her lips, which irked me. Thank goodness the Widow was with Father collecting an errant lamb who escaped the fencing and Cassie was still asleep.

"Me thinks I know where your affections are headed. Perhaps a little birdie told me. Perhaps I have known for some time."

"Birdie, nonsense," I shot back. "The only way you could possibly know is from reading my diary and that is unforgivable. Never, not once have I snooped into your personal belongings. Really, Abbey, all I can say is that you and Billy deserve each other. And if you do know something from reading my diary, you had best keep your mouth quiet." My hiding place would now have to be moved and I would have to become more circumspect with what I wrote. Things have a way of coming to light even when one is cautious.

"Ella, I promise you. I will not speak a word of what I know. I have been tested by outrage and felt its hard slap and do not want it to strike one of my sisters." She put down her spoon and reached for my hand and held it. She looked most earnestly into my eyes and said, "It will be difficult for you if you do take up with him, even more difficult than Billy's and my indiscretion. You well know how the townsfolk discourage young women from attraction to the original peoples. There are too many barriers—a whole way of life so opposite from ours. You also well know the stories of those women who took up a life with them."

I did know of what she spoke. I too have seen women ostracized by the entire community and set out alone in a life of great hardship—a life they held no prior knowledge of. But what Abbey does not know is that nothing will come of my affections. There are my dreams of a future, of becoming either a doctor or a poet. That she does not know. That I forbid myself to write in words because those very words, that very intent is branded only to my heart.

Abbey proved a good side to her nature. She said nothing of that night or what she read in my diary and for that my heart was renewed with hope for her. No person is all bad and I never really thought Abbey anything but the goodness made by our mother and father. She perhaps has chosen a man to spend her life with that might not be worthy of her, but then again, people change—even Billy could transform himself into a just and fit man and surprise us. Most people are shaped by the land and the hours. Have I not seen that first hand? Has the Widow not become a kinder woman who occasionally tips her hat in friendship towards one of us?

She knew Cassie so longed for a cut of lovely dress material she saw in the seamstress shop in River John and with the money the Widow had saved, she went straight into town and bought it. Not only did she buy the lace and flower printed cotton, she also made it into a summer dress for Cassie. As she took up the hem, Cassie standing on the deacon's bench, I saw my mother's hands as she carefully pin up the hem for one of us.

Life is a circle. Sweetness swings back when we least expect it.

IN THE HEART OF THE WIGWAM

The Micmac people become intrigued with the surrey and I allow the children to sit on the three seat bench, their faces sweet in delight. Gabby is tethered to a nearby tree and is being of good temperament. She has shown no usual signs of a restless nature. It is as though she were kin to them. The women stroke the side of my surrey and reach high on tiptoes to touch its sun shield which must look like a bonnet to them. They also finger the door latch as though it were a jewel from a faraway land.

It is most interesting to watch—all the things I have taken for granted become a marvel to them. Never have I seen the Micmac people do this when they travel into River John to sell wampum beads and porcupine quillwork. But on their own land they feel safe enough to explore my belongings and the surrey has fascinated the two women.

Here, the women wear a mixture of their own clothing and ones they traded or bartered for with the Europeans. They wear moccasins and the younger women have on blouses decorated in lovely beadwork. Their hair is long and unfettered but two old women who sit outside a wigwam have their hair plaited into braids and wear their pointed hats on their heads, even in the heat. The seated women work beads into art and scowl as they look my way, chatting a language not understood by myself. Most of the men, I assume, must be at the shores fishing or out on the ocean in their birch-bark canoes—only a few old men in the Micmac village idly sit smoking their pipes, and a few younger men, shirtless with tobacco pouches of moose skin bound to their waists are busy stretching hides.

"What do you want here?" one of the women asks. She is no longer interested in stroking the surrey and eyes me with great curiosity which is tinted with a slight look of disdain.

Father has told me that the Micmac as well as other original people have great suspicion of the settlers and that their mistrust is well founded. Even though they stand quite close to me their eyes seem far away, nearly in another land quite foreign to me.

I look back at the children gathered at the surrey. Gabby neighs and loves the attention the youngsters show her. Seldom does she stand so still for children, her memory of the MacKay neighbors' children, their taunting abuse, still fresh in Gabby's mind.

The young woman again asks, "What do you want?" My attention snaps back to matters at hand. I tell her that Stands Like a Tree needs a canoe hidden at Caijebouguac and that they must hurry. His life is at stake and he is in great peril.

"Also, my friend Minnie is recovering here and I would like to see her."

They look at one another and nod. It is my good fortune to have stumbled upon two who speak some English. Because I have not stressed hard enough the great danger that Stands Like a Tree might be in, I repeat the urgency of his request.

"The Mohawks are on Stands Like a Tree's trail. He needs his people to hide a canoe underneath willows and eel grass at the head of the bay near the rock pilings." The day is hot and my patience wanes with the sun drumming hard upon my head.

The women look at one another and the younger one breaks into a run towards the old men smoking pipes. She runs throughout the village yelling, "Stands Like a Tree needs help," and soon a band of very young men gather. She turns and points at me and they nod at me and then disperse.

"I will take you to the woman called Minnie, friend of our village. She is known as Good Woman Minnie. We, the First Nation People, find hope in your kind through her fine example."

She speaks very clearly and I ask her where she learned English.

"The missionaries taught me these words. We have no quarrel with them. They schooled some of the children you see here. In exchange we gave them much prized beaver pelts, but they are hard to find now. Too many people shoot them and the waters where beavers build their dams cry out with loss of those once plentiful wooden tails." She does not look me in the eye for fear I might enter her soul. I have seen this before when the Micmacs come into town to barter.

If only she knew it is on account of an ill-mannered French man that Stands Like a Tree is now being tracked and hunted.

"Follow me," she says and walks at a rapid pace to the largest wigwam. Around it are several smaller ones, birch bark peeling back. I marvel their ingenuity—homes that can be erected within an hour's time—bark sheets that can be rolled up and easily carried to the next settlement as weather changes.

With the moose hide flap pulled back, Minnie is clearly visible. She is seated on a spruce mat and her white hair hangs loose. Unable to contain my happiness I run to her and hug her with a fierceness I thought myself incapable of.

"What is on your arms and face?"

"Ella, I am so grateful you came. It is a healing cream the people here made for my scratches and scrapes; fir balsam to help my skin heal faster. An old woman's skin is like parchment paper. It tears easily and tree branches have long, sharp fingers." She laughs at her remark.

"They also gave me flagroot, or Ki'kwesu'sk, as they call it, to calm down my liver which seems to have had a bad temper tantrum. It is terrible tasting stuff, thick and muddy all the way down." She makes a face when describing it. "Mina, over there, set my arm-bone with eel skin. See, it is almost good as new."

"But, Ella, I tell you true, there are not a kinder people on the face of the earth than my Micmac family. They called upon the Spirit, Helper Bear, to carry me over and past my fright which was worse than my scrapes and aches." She paused and brushed her hair aside. "I could not sleep the first couple of nights, so Mina slept with me." I looked at the woman Mina working on her basket, her eyes intent on the weave she worked, bunches of sweetgrass nearby.

"It is not an easy thing to witness someone's scalping. So much blood. So much blood. I tried to put myself between the Mohawk chief and the French man. But the chief shoved me aside. My arm snapped like an old stick. Getting away was my only thought and I broke into a run so fast even the moose munching on flag root looked shocked when they saw me career past them."

"Oh, Minnie, I am terribly sorry. It pains my heart to think of the horror you witnessed." I took her into my arms as though she were my small child and held her.

"Thank goodness and glad tidings that Stands Like a Tree found me asleep underneath a spruce, insects taking over my body as though it were a better home than the ground."

"You are safe now," I said and cuddled her close.

"And, how is our friend?" Minnie inquired.

"He is in some danger from the Mohawks. He was told not to follow them to the fort but he worried for your safety. They promised not to harm you and had said their quarrel was not with you, rather it was the thief who stole their rare, white sable."

Mina, the other woman present, who is about Minnie's age, left carrying the basket with her, as well as an armful of forest grasses.

"Have I offended her?" I ask Minne.

"No, she just wants to give us privacy. These people are most courteous. So, will Stands Like a Tree be safe?"

"The Micmac people will take a canoe to the bay where he can escape to Cape Breton. They cannot follow him there." I did not tell her my fears for his safety. No, Minnie had much to contend with—the loss of her home and her ordeal at the fort.

"Minnie, I could not wait to tell you, but my Aunt Kathleen has offered you a room in her house in Tatamagouche. She is most eager to have you live with her since she finds herself lonely. Her children seldom visit. They are busy with work."

"No thanks, Ella. Tell your aunt I am honored she would have me, but I intend to stay put here for now. These are my people too and I have much to learn from them."

Sadness swelled in my heart. Here was Minnie with nothing but her name, her house gone, and still no self-pity in the woman. Yet, I fret over the simplest things, sisters that tease one another and me, worries about what to do with my future. Clearly, I have some work cut out if I am to whittle my soul into the finest representation of a human being.

Minnie yawns and says she is in need of rest. Before I leave she asks me one heart wrenching question.

"Is there nothing left? What of my letters from Mr. Miller that were in the attic?"

"I fear nothing of the house survived. But I promise you I will take a rake and comb through the ashes. If I find something you will be the very first to know. As you are probably aware, both your out-house and barn survived."

"Go now child. I am weary." Her face was drawn and in the light I could easily see her jaundiced skin. She was frail, yet her eyes shone bright as always. She would from that day forward be my "always." Minnie Always I would call her.

Ever so softly I kissed her brow, ran my hand down her cheek and left. I did not look back. If I had, it would have been too difficult to take my leave. Outside the sun was slowly slipping down the spin of the day.

Gabby swished her tail, tossed her mane as I neared. The children were gone too, so Gabby and I quietly left the place of the Micmac people.

And life seemed heavy at the moment.

COMBING THE RUINS

"This Minnie Miller must be an important woman to you, Ella," Abbey says as we comb through the ashes. "You have certainly spent much time with her and even more time fretting over her."

The day beats hot on our backs and the humidity is horrendous. Dust rises from each poke in the soil and large stones from the hearth snag the rakes. Bits of crockery and glass slowly emerge and it is my hope to find something that will be significant to Minnie. Given the last several days, there is much to meditate on as we search the ash.

"Yes, she is an angel to me. There is no way to explain my attachment to her other than there is an invisible thread binds us heart to heart."

Abbey wears our Mother's old beehive bonnet, tied underneath the chin, the bonnet Mother used to wear gardening. We are reduced to our bloomers and blouses, our skirts hung on a post near the well. Earlier, I dipped a handkerchief in the well water and tied it around my neck with the hopes it would offer relief. The trickles of water slide down my back and between my breasts giving me momentary reprieve from the heat. It is one of those days wherein one feels with certainty a fiery storm with lots of lightning will break through—the humidity like a landed cloud.

"Do you think we will find anything?" Abbey asks.

"I hope so, for Minnie's sake."

Abbey is to be married to Billy in two weeks and the Widow Applegate has again surprised us with wedding plans, a church supper and another new dress for Abbey made of pure rose satin that the Widow herself is stitching for her. Occasionally now, we call her by her rightful name, Elizabeth. She insists on Mrs. Elizabeth and of course we never call her Mother, and we never call her the Widow to her face, although I did once slip but she must not have heard me.

"On the day we marry, I should weigh next to nothing after combing through this in such heat," Abbey remarks. I can believe it as sweat pours off my face.

"Ella, why do you think there was so much trouble between us? Was I a bad sister?"

Her words, the boldness of them, take me aback. I suppose raking through these ashes is symbolic of raking through who we have been towards one another.

"No, you have not been a bad sister, just irksome at times. Perhaps it was hard for you to have me as an older sister. Bossy should have been my middle name."

"It is not that, Ella. It seems both Father and Mother always gave you a special place as the first born child in the family. It is clear that Father greatly admires you because you are so smart and have such an independent spirit. It has always seemed that you carried more authority in the house and I resented that. Do you have any idea how much authority costs if one has it and the other does not? Especially as girls? It has cost me my entire pride." She wipes sweat off her face and this spreads the ash dust from the ground across her cheeks. "They always listened to you, but not to me."

"Abbey, you should just see yourself," and I break out in laughter at the sight of her. "You know that gray mule the MacKay family owns?"

"Yes, I know that ornery beast that brays like a sick kid, why?"

"Well, you look gray as their mule. Come here, sister. I will wipe the ash off your face. You should see yourself. I bet Billy would laugh at his bride-to-be if he could see you now."

With my neck handkerchief still wet, I carefully wipe off the ash, the creases around her pert nose. There is a sad melancholy to her face, one I have not before noticed. Her eyes are like opals. Perhaps, I too have shorted her of affection, busy with my own projects and with Minnie. Perhaps I should have tendered more care towards her after the death of our mother. But it is hard to know the needs of others, especially if they cover them up and hide behind bad behavior.

"Abbey, I am sorry for any way I may have hurt you. That was not my intent. There is nothing I can do about being the first child. Not a thing. Both you and Cassie have made my life less lonely. I cannot imagine a childhood here in River John without the company of sisters. Let us get on with this raking before the sky opens into a downpour."

But Abbey is intent on settling things. This must be a direct result to her starting out on a new life—wanting to clear the old.

She continues. "I have, at times, quite admittedly, been jealous of you. You must have noticed that, especially when I stole Billy from you."

"You did not steal him." I put a special emphasis on *steal*. "I wanted nothing more to do with him. Besides, there is much an older sister notices but refrains from speaking. I would have looked most vain had I spoken to you about jealousy—just the mere mention of the word would have set you off. And would you have believed me if I had said you were the jealous one, not me? No, you needed to come to it in your own time and on your own terms."

"Ella, I am most frightened by the prospect of marriage, but given our overnight in Tatamagouche there was no other alternative. We needed to come clean in the face of the community. But, I fear my life will become as a still-born. There is much loneliness our mother endured after she wed Father, especially before we children arrived. He was off to Halifax many a time purchasing tools for his shop or things for the farm."

"How do you know that, Abbey?"

"She spoke to me about it. In a town like West Branch River John, especially way out where we live, there is little by way of social life, except an occasional event at the Kirk, and the winters are long and hard. She sometimes pined for life in Scotland. She told me so. It was nearly communal back in the highlands with several families living together. One had little chance to feel lonely with music, dance and festive family gatherings. Now people live further apart and see less of each other."

"How could you possibly doubt your importance in the family when she confided such loneliness to you? Do you not see how she trusted you? She never, not once, spoke to me of such things. You will do fine in marriage, Abbey. You have many friends in town."

"Ella, I am sorry for being difficult, and I am most sorry for reading parts of your diary. Will you accept my apology?"

"You need not ask. You know I will."

I took her in my arms, there in the heat of the sun, the field's grasses aflutter in the building breeze, but I did not hold her long as thunder and lightning struck a fit in the air. Just as we were about to rush to Minnie's barn something shone from underneath a charred piece of wood. I quickly picked it up as we headed for shelter.

"What do you think is in that tinder box, Ella?" Abbey scratched her nose and pushed her hair back.

Outside the barn, everything began to refresh itself in the cool rain, the air charged with power. It poured with a fierceness not seen all summer long and if the lightning subsided we declared we would strip and run outside in the downpour. There was no one to be seen for miles and we occasionally did this back at home. *Rain will ruin them*, Mother always used to say, but we, of course, have ceased doing this with Mrs. Elizabeth present in our home.

"Let us have a look at the tinder box." I turned the small, attached key and opened the box. Inside, rested a gold wedding band and an odd broach of some sort and some land papers, grantees, signed by Mr. Miller himself.

"It is a cameo broach, Ella. A most beautiful cameo made with pearl or ivory set in a gold background. I wager Mr. Miller gave that to your friend, Minnie. What do you think?"

"You are possibly right. And here is a lock of hair which I suspect was clipped from their baby who died." We will stow it away on that rafter until I can take it to Minnie.

"What a surprise and what delight she will undoubtedly feel that this has been recovered," Abbey noted.

"Let us peel off our damp clothes now that the lightning has sub-sided and dance in the rain."

"By Jove, that is a great idea."

Abbey's body was white as the inside of a clam shell. She lifted her face as though baptized by rain and never had I seen a more pure looking soul, emptied entirely of herself so that only pure essence remained. Her wet hair snaked down her back and she reached for my hands as we danced, each of us singing songs from our mother's homeland, songs that she once sang to us. It was as though she was here, dancing with us, and as if Abbey knew my very thoughts, we dropped one hand each and reached out to the spirit of our mother who now danced with her daughters in the rain.

Certainly, this moment, earned through pain and grief, was something to carry into my future. When days got dark, I would take sustenance in what was—a dance with my sister, Abbey, on Minnie's land—a time when our mother also joined us. And were we not our-selves now joined in the harmony of sisterhood? And was it not in itself a marriage of two spirits made whole?

A Gift for Minnie

You cannot imagine my elation when the townsfolk and the Micmac people all came together to make a home for Minnie. It was a harmonious joining of two distinct peoples for the benefit of a woman who lost the home she and her husband long ago built. The Micmac people erected two wigwams joined together with a cut-out door between the two. One wigwam would be Minnie's kitchen and storage, the other her sleeping quarters and living area.

In the first wigwam, five spruce poles were lashed together at the top with a split black spruce root. Then the spruce poles were spread out at the bottom on the earth. A moosewood hoop was tied underneath the poles to brace them. Shorter poles were tied to the hoop to become support for the birchbark cover, which Minnie requested be double wrapped. Then the birchbark was laid over the poles like shingles, starting from the bottom and worked upward. This would effectively repel the rain. Some extra poles were laid out to help hold the birch sheets in place and then they were tied down with spruce root. There was a small opening in the top of the first wigwam in order to let smoke escape, but it would be covered with a bark collar when the days grew colder. A young Micmac volunteered to put the bark collar on come winter and he would leave a small opening for the smoke to escape. No one wanted Minnie up on a ladder to put the collar in place, especially after all she had been through.

Father was amongst those townspeople helping with the building of Minnie's new home. He insisted that slate from a nearby quarry be used for the flooring because it held the heat better once the woodstove hauled here from Dartmouth was in use. He and several other men made numerous trips to the quarry and worked the stone into the earth, packed it hard with dirt, so there was a flat surface for Minnie to walk upon in her home. It was unheard of in these parts to have a slate floor in a wigwam, but this was done entirely for Minnie's sake.

Over this slate flooring, the town's women placed two rag rugs they had hooked—one for each room in Minnie's new place. Furniture, a table and two chairs, a deacon's bench and a wonderful pine post bed frame were made by Father and his friends. Mrs. Elizabeth and Pastor Smith's wife, Hattie, stitched together tacking for a feather mattress and made quilts for Minnie's bed. The Micmac people gave her a moose hide which would keep her warm on bitter cold days. Many donations poured in: crockery pots, dishes, two tin cups, a steamer trunk for Minnie's clothes and lanterns as well as candles arrived.

Once in place, the colorful quilts on the bed, a cup of wildflowers on the table, a red ribbon on the butter churn handle, Minnie's new place revealed charm. Of course, she was back in the Micmac settlement and thought only the wigwams themselves were erected at her place. She knew nothing about the floor, furnishings, and the contributions from both the River John community and the Micmac settlement. There was talk that even the Mohawks donated a lucky door hanging made of bone. It suddenly appeared out of nowhere.

Luckily, this new home was close to the springhouse so Minnie would not have far to travel for her water. Also, there was a good stand of oak trees close by and a few chestnut trees and they would break the heavy winds. The best part for my friend's new dwelling was a newly built white picket fence, the old weathered one torn down. The new one circled her home. Upon it was strung a banner which said, "Welcome Home, Mrs. Miller." The men folk cut her wood for the winter and stacked next to the springhouse which had a substantial overhang to keep it dry. Since the wood was not seasoned, they also donated five cords of wood cut two years back from their own properties.

Upon the table I placed the tinder box. Minnie did not know of its find and the box was meant as a surprise. This was the house Minnie always requested. She said, "I do not need something so durable it lasts years. I am old and need shelter for but a short while. The roundness of the wigwam will give me great comfort—in my circle many friends and many memories will visit. A circle is the most complete form on earth. Because of that, I want to live in the center of a circle."

Where Water is Split

The following summer I walked to the bay where Stands Like a Tree took his leave. Word was that he, indeed, escaped the Mohawk's wrath. Word also had it that he now lives in Cape Breton and teaches the Micmac people's children how to read. He once said it was important to move as the world moved, which included gathering tools needed in a world that depended more and more on the written word. His was a culture that had always relied on the oral tradition, but that was changing with the advent of more settlers. It warmed my heart to know he was safe and that a good life unfolded before him.

I imagined his cutting through water as he escaped, the canoe's paddle dipping into the blue dark, his hair fanned in the breeze. It seemed I could see his muscles as he paddled, the breadth of his shoulders as he headed into the quiet unknown. From shore I watched what I could only imagine; the spirit of water guiding him into open water. The water would become his mother, the one torn from him so long ago and who died from grief when he was taken from her.

Behind his humped-back canoe, the water split. Two cords of water to the left, two cords to the right. And in that split rests what is most sacred on earth—the blue mystery one attempts to understand. In that attempt one makes right from life. In the deep unknowing something becomes known if one dare search. For it is the prompt which helps one arrive upon the shore of self-understanding.

I do not know if I will ever again see my friend, Stands Like a Tree. Yet, I feel his presence as though he were somehow part of me.

Sometimes I hear him say, "Ella, Ella," like that night in the dark when those words carried scent of sweet grass. I inhale deeply at such times and a wave of great tenderness fills me.

I must, as before, go forward as one unseen and meditate upon thoughts that bother me. For instance, in the forest God comes to me. In church, he completely vanishes. And then there are questions as to why God is considered a man and not a woman. It seems totally unjust and bothers me, although I speak nothing of such matters to my family. Furthermore, when I think of the names that depict our sex, I become even more troubled. Why is there a man at the end of woman? Why is there a man in human? Certainly, men are the ones who invented the English language and they did so with themselves in mind and ordained everything as man-made. But it is from the womb of woman that all life bursts forth.

But, for now, my thoughts veer primarily towards attending The University of Kings College. I will have to cut my hair very short and be as a young man, clothes and all. With myself shorn of hair, a great transformation will likely occur. I expect this change will extract a price. It will be a falsehood of the greatest magnitude. But I live in a time when women are not allowed such opportunity as an education.

To prepare for university, I have even taken the letters from my first name and concluded my new name will be Al MacKinnon, short for Allen. Knock off the n and there is an Ella in Allen if you read the name backwards.

Ahead are both trauma and challenges. Ahead is unimaginable hardship.

From the next book by Dianna Henning...

Chapter 1

There I was standing before a smoky mirror in my new lodgings at the boarding house, neighboring The University of Kings College. My hat hid my tucked under hair when I paid for my boarding and I was dressed in a pea jacket and gray breeches. For all anyone could tell I was a young man through and through. But inside myself, I felt entirely woman. Ella, I said, you are now Al. My jacket slid off easily and I tossed it on the bed. The shears were cold as the legtrap years back. My hand trembled as I cut great swaths of hair. It seemed as though I erased my entire being as I cut closer and closer to my head. Into a muslin bag I stuffed all the cut hair to later toss in the forest. As I stood looking at my newly created self, tears flooded my face and I threw myself onto the bed and cried as never before. I cannot do it, I said. It is forbidden that girls attend university.

Author's Note

Author photo: Jody Wright

DIANNA HENNING holds a Master of Fine Arts in Writing from Vermont College of Fine Arts. She has published in many literary magazines. She taught creative writing for *California Poets in the Schools,* through the *William James Association's Prison Arts Program* and through several *California Arts Council* grants, and was a co-recipient of a '08 *California Humanities Stories Grant.* Dianna has been twice nominated for a Pushcart Prize. Her most recent book, *The Broken Bone Tongue 2009,* was published by *Black Buzzard Press,* Austin TX. Dianna's work has appeared in, in part: *Crazyhorse, The Lullwater Review, Poetry International, Fugue, Swink, The Asheville Poetry Review, South Dakota Review, Hawai'i Pacific Review* and *The Seattle Review.* She lives in Lassen County, California, with her husband Kam and malamute Sakari—here she finds inspiration in the vast stretches of land, the ponderosa trees and abundant wild life. The sheer beauty of the place never fails to amaze her.